Nun's Drift

Four Stories, One Community

Sheila Jacobs

malcolm down

PUBLISHING

First published 2024 by Malcolm Down Publishing Ltd
www.malcolmdown.co.uk

28 27 26 25 24   7 6 5 4 3 2 1

British Library Cataloguing in Publication Data
A catalogue record for this book is available from the British Library.

ISBN 978-1-915046-97-0

Cover design by Esther Kotecha
Art direction by Sarah Grace

Printed in the UK

Season icons designed by Freepik

Dedication

All that we have accomplished, you have done for us.

(Isaiah 26:12, NIV)

Thanks

To Caroline Griffiths
and
Helen Hudson

For my dad, Keith Jacobs,
Phil Steward, Maria Redmond,
Dennis Barton and the cast of Grassmore Green.

Contents

Introduction

I first had the idea for this story's setting when I went to a steam rally one summer's day with my friend Helen Hudson. It was held in an idyllic village. I knew I wanted to write a novel based in such a place, and call it *Nun's Drift*. Later, Caroline Griffiths, my childhood friend, persuaded me to write more fiction – I'd been writing non-fiction, and editing, and hadn't written a novel in years. The short story I wrote for her turned into this book.

Nun's Drift is about four people, intertwined, and yet separate; a story of forgiveness and hope, of running away and peace, of doubt and joy, of perspectives and love. It's a story of second chances, of motivations, of brokenness and restoration.

I hope you enjoy reading it as much as I've enjoyed writing it.

Sheila Jacobs
Halstead, autumn 2024

Author's note:
Rosemary's 'words from the Bible' are from the famous chapter about love, 1 Corinthians 13.

PART ONE

Meg's Story
Forgiveness

Unreal. Never thought I'd be here again.

Drawing into the station, train slowing down, life slowing down. Familiar fields and meadows and now the platform . . .

I manage to get to my feet, reluctant to grab my bag from the rack. Feeling every step an effort, I'm unable to smile at the guy who lets me go in front of him. Can't even be bothered to say thanks.

Now here I am, on the platform. It's been years. Seven, to be exact. Seven years since I was last in Nun's Drift.

Sitting on the bench, waiting, the May sunshine warms my face. Alright, the air seems cleaner than it does at home. It always did. Every summer as kids, we'd come here, Micky and me, and spend happy weeks watching the farmer combining – good old Tony Martin with the bushy beard – darting among the straw bales, chasing huge dragonflies and eating warm cheese and juicy tomatoes among the cornfields. Long time ago. And of course, I lived here as a teenager.

They've got flower baskets dangling prettily from the station buildings. Pansies. Later in the year, it'll be petunias. They have gorgeous summer gardens in Nun's Drift, a couple of miles away from the station at Howfield Cross, crammed full of vibrant geraniums and all sorts of dahlias. I remember the gardening club in the village is very active. They know how to live an exciting life.

I recognise her straight away. She's not into technology, my aunty Lou, so there hasn't been any Facetime or Zoom, WhatsApp or Facebook, but she doesn't look that much different. She's fifty now; blonde hair, bobbed, lighter, I think because it's streaked with grey, but she's got the same big smile and too-tight jeans for an older lady.

'You haven't changed,' I say, as I hug her.

'You have,' she replies. 'Too thin!'

Same old Land Rover, gathering moss. I climb into the car. 'If you're still selling all those cakes,' I say, 'I suppose...'

'Oh, yes – we'll be feeding you up!' She presses her foot down and the engine roars. 'Too scrawny!'

She flashes me a sudden smile, reaches over and squeezes my shoulder. 'I'm glad you're here. You need Nun's Drift, Meg.' She gives me a knowing look, crashes the gears and utters a word I didn't know she used.

I sigh. It was all Dad's idea. He'd sent me to his sister once before, when he thought I needed a bit of help. I was nineteen then. I guess I never learned my lesson. I'm back in Nun's Drift for another one.

We're out of the Howfields, the indicator's on, and we turn left by a grassy island triangle onto the Fairleigh Road, which leads into Nun's Drift. I start a little as I spot the ubiquitous new-builds on what used to be a large field with a derelict barn. One glance at my aunt tells me that it isn't a popular addition to the village. We cross the bridge over the little river, and pass the playing field. I notice a new pavilion. The main street – unimaginatively named 'Church Street' – is as quiet as I remember it.

'The bank's gone.'

'And the post office. There's one in the Co-op now – Stile Road. We had a petition, but . . .' My aunt crashes the gears again and frowns. 'There's something wrong with this thing! I'll have to get Tony to look at it.'

'Ah, Tony! Always getting a round in at the pub!' She shoots me a sharp glance. 'Is he OK, then?' I ask, a bit lamely.

'Fine.' Her tone is surprisingly terse.

I see the vets, a hairdresser, an antique shop and the hardware store; the doctor's surgery, *Vanity Designs* (how does Daisy Parker keep going? Massively overpriced clothing) and St Saviour's, looming in the background, castle-like, with its square tower. I wonder if they still ring the bells on Wednesday evenings. *Intrusive.*

We stop before we reach the foot of the hill.

'The butcher's gone . . . Mr Measly, wasn't it?'

She pulls on the handbrake with what seems an enormous effort. 'We've got a farm shop at the Thompson-Traceys', so Mr *Moseley* sells his delightful products there.'

We've stopped by the tearoom, opposite the village green, with its big pond and many ducks. The horse chestnut tree by the Half Moon – the sign still looks tatty – is clothed in spring freshness, but autumn brings the biggest, brightest conkers. I remember they do good beer-battered cod and chips in the Half Moon. Or they used to.

I pause for a moment and admire the view; the green is dotted with so many daisies it's like a mini snow drift.

I get out before my aunt questions me some more about my weight. The sun is shining, the sky is blue. There's purple wisteria around the café door. It's idyllic. Of course it is, it's Nun's Drift. For a moment, I think about the word 'drift'. Is the village named because of the drift of daisies? Where does the nun fit in? Did she drift? Why? And where to?

My aunt insists on carrying my bag. Walking into the café, it's the same tinkling bell as I remember from my younger days. It's bizarre. There are two elderly ladies sitting at one of the little tables. They look like the same tables from years ago. They might even be the same ladies, just seven years older. Like me. I watch them eat their scones, slapping on wads of jam. *The cups and saucers still don't match.*

My aunt's struggling with my bag. I adjust my backpack and insist on taking the weight of my own luggage. I suppose there's deep significance in that.

There's a girl, late teens, I guess, behind the counter. She smiles at me. It's a friendly smile but she looks a bit nervous. *What does she know?* I'm on guard.

'This is Cornelia,' says Aunty Lou.

'Hello, Meg.' Her voice has a Suffolk lilt; she has brown hair, tied up in a loose bun. She twists a tea towel in her hand. She doesn't seem to know what to say next.

'Is Polly still here?' I ask, glancing around at the familiar shelves, the pretty plates, the quaint teapots. There's a wonderful aroma of fattening cakes.

'No,' says my aunt. 'She lives in Ipswich now.'

'Wow, the big city!' I exclaim. There's a giggle from Cornelia.

'Well,' she says. 'It is, really, up to Nun's Drift.'

I sigh heavily. Has she ever been to London?

'Rosemary's still around,' says my aunt.

Rosemary's my aunt's friend. I've always found it amusing that her surname is Lane. Sounds more like a place than a person.

'Meg!' My aunt's voice slices through my quietness, which has followed the sigh. Is she about to tell me off – have a go at what she used to call my 'attitude'? I let my eyes wander round the café; then I meet her steady gaze. She jerks her head towards a high shelf. 'I'm going to need some help getting up there. Three rungs up a ladder and I'm useless. You know I got stuck up the church bell tower? Took two beefy men to bring me down – not the worst moment of my life.' She gives me a cheeky wink. 'Anyway, while you're here, you can make yourself useful, and I remember you're good with heights. See the Spode jug? I'm going to sell that, but I'm not getting stuck—'

'I can do that for you.' Someone has come through from the kitchen. Tall, lean, fair, around thirty. He puts a box down behind the counter and I notice that Cornelia's face reddens. He glances at her, and then he notices me. I have a strange feeling I've seen him somewhere before.

'My niece, Meg,' says my aunt, a bit too casually, I think. She looks at me and the look has a warning.

He nods; there's no friendly hello. I recognise a familiar cool, appraising detachment. I hope my face reflects a lack of interest.

'Got to dash, Louisa,' he says. 'Be back later.'

His voice is firm but light.

I wish I could have a cigarette, but remember what my aunt thinks of smoking. Anyway, it's time I quit.

'And I'll bring my stepladder and get to that shelf, OK?'

'Excellent.' She frowns as he pushes past her. 'Don't do anything I wouldn't do.'

He's grinning. It's an attractive grin, slightly crooked. Even the old ladies watch him leave the café.

'Who's that?' I put my luggage down.

'That's Barny,' says Aunty Lou, briskly.

I watch him from the little square-paned window, crossing the road. My aunt notices.

'Meg . . .'

'Oh, don't worry,' I say, too bluntly.

My aunt suddenly squeezes my arm in what I assume is a reassuring gesture, and I feel irritated.

She turns away as the bell tinkles again. A customer walks in, huffing and puffing and asking for cakes, even though it looks as if she's already eaten too many that morning. My aunt talks to the customer. I sit down on one of the rickety chairs and stare at the little jar of flowers and the floral patterns on plates on the shelf beside me.

'She's so 'appy you're 'ere, you know,' says Cornelia, quietly wiping down a nearby table.

'Sorry?'

'Your aunt. She's been lookin' forward to seein' you.'

I'm still annoyed, but she's being so nice.

'I bet you'd like a cup of tea,' she says, helpfully.

'I'd like a smoke.'

'Oh. Your aunt . . .'

'Yeah, yeah. Tea's fine.'

'We've got chamomile, lemon . . .'

'The usual brown breakfast stuff's OK for me, thanks.'

I hope she'll go away. I so don't want to talk. But she leans towards me and whispers, conspiratorially, 'You've met the mystery man.'

'What?'

Her cheeks are still flushed. I haven't got the strength or the interest to continue the conversation, but maybe Barny is one of Cornelia's pet subjects. Perhaps he's one of *everyone's* pet subjects in this village.

'Well, 'e's a bit mysterious, like.'

'So you said.' I lean back and hear an ominous 'crack'. She doesn't seem to notice. I decide not to mention it. I can't risk getting told off for breaking something on my first day here. And the thought of that makes me feel about five years old.

'Just turned up, from nowhere. Won't say where 'e's from. Got a bit of a past, I reckon.'

'Haven't we all?' But catching her wide-eyed gaze, I think she probably hasn't.

She looks down, and she's blushing again.

Without warning, the familiar flood of longing and sadness almost overwhelms me. *Oh, Micky. Where are you? Everything reminds me of you.*

Maybe she sees a change in my expression, but Cornelia pulls out a chair; it scrapes on the tiles and the headache I'm feeling at the back of my eyes worsens. I'm never going to get that tea. She leans forward and I realise that she has a sweetness in her hazel eyes.

'I don't know you and you don't know me, yet, but I 'ope we can be friends.'

Really? I wonder again how much she knows about me.

'We've got the fair comin' up. Traction engines, all that. We'll 'ave a great time.'

I remember the fair – all ceramic tat and old cars. 'Yeah.' Then I can't help but add, and my voice sounds cynical even to my own ears, 'It's a wonderful life.'

'It is. It's a simple life in Nun's Drift. It ain't for everyone but it suits me.'

'I don't remember you from when I was here before.'

'Oh, I've only been around just over a year. I live with my uncle. Life's better 'ere,' she says, thoughtfully. 'It's not like the world outside. It's special. Different.'

I realise I'm staring. Does she know about Micky? Yes, she must do. Or is she thinking about that at all? No, she isn't thinking about me, or about Micky; she's caught up in some romantic idyll. I suddenly remember, with a twinge of sickness, when I was like her.

She clears her throat and stands up. 'I'll get your tea.'

'And I'll look forward to the traction engines.'

Her voice is all bright and cheerful now. 'My uncle's got one.'

'Got one what?' It suddenly registers. 'Your uncle's Tony – the farmer?'

'Yes, your aunt's boyfriend.'

'Tony? He's not her boyfriend,' I say, with a small laugh. 'They've been friends for years. Besides, he's married. Or got a partner.' I stop talking. Commitment to someone else doesn't mean people don't mess around.

'Nah, she left him, she did, 'is partner, and we don't know why. Got another fella, I reckon. Ages ago now. She sorta just upped and went, not even a note. Came downstairs one mornin', car was gone, and she never came back. 'E don't talk about it. I come to live with 'im because my mum said it would do us both good . . . 'E got very down, you know. And 'e was all alone, and my mum said, all them shotguns, let's keep an eye on 'im . . . Anyway, 'e's alright now.'

'He's not my aunt's *boyfriend*,' I repeat, slowly. I can feel myself frowning. Something in me needs to know.

She wrinkles her nose. 'Well, *somethin's* going on.'

My aunt's fifty, and Tony must be pushing sixty. Suddenly, I feel very tired. I thought I'd come to Nun's Drift to get away from relationships, and the devastation they can cause. *Oh, Micky, I'm sorry.* Rushing water; a river with bursting banks. *Micky!* A car, red tail lights in the fog, the driver just a silhouette. *You're alive, I just know it. Please come back.*

Later, Cornelia tells me, over a sneaky cigarette, what Barny made of me on that first encounter – and, apparently, his continuing evaluation.

"E thinks you're a moody cow,' she says.

'I don't care,' I reply, and am surprised to find that I do.

The next evening, we're in my aunt's tiny living room eating shop-bought lasagne off trays on our laps. Tony's there, laughing as my aunt tops up his glass. Likes a bit of red, does Tony. His face is tanned and deeply lined from exposure to the elements and – probably – abandonment. But he's much more relaxed than I remember. Perhaps it's the wine. Or maybe the single life suits him.

I notice his beard is more than flecked with grey, but it's well-trimmed. As he reaches to a side table for another bread roll, I notice the muscular arms. He isn't in bad shape for an oldie.

Cornelia is laughing too, and everything is very merry. My aunt observes that it's a pity it's raining or we could have sat outside on the patio. The rest of us snigger. The patio is half a dozen slabs out back, a small courtyard with a few flowerpots facing an old broken fence and a *lot* of brambles. Tony says he must get round to clearing it, because those few chairs and crummy tables she puts outside the shop on the pavement in summer would be better round the back. Aunty Lou shakes her head and says he's been saying that for years and the brambles are never cleared. He points out that farming's busy work. She says he hasn't even fixed the gate, so how could people sit round back, even if it was cleared? He says she's nagging him again. But there's no malice. He's teasing. She slaps his bulky shoulder playfully and says he spends too much time doing up that old wreck of a traction engine. They joke for a bit about 'old wrecks'.

Cornelia's right. Something's going on.

I watch the rain slide down the little window in the kitchen as I wash up the plates. The flat above the shop is cramped, but it's cosy. I feel a strange sensation creep over me and realise that for the first time in months, I'm relaxing.

We have strong coffee, mostly because Tony's getting tipsy. Aunty Lou excuses herself and heads for the bathroom. I wonder if she's a bit tipsy too.

While she's gone, Tony leans towards his niece.

'You need to be careful, my girl. Don't want to come after anyone with my shotgun.'

'Don't worry, Uncle Tony,' she says, primly. 'I can take care of myself.'

He roars with laughter. 'Not with that one.'

'Everyone deserves a second chance,' she says, firmly.

Is that true?

Tony voices my doubt. His voice is raised and rather slurred. 'What's he done that he *needs* a second chance, then? Eh? Come on. I want to know. What's he done? Murdered someone?'

There's no reply from his tight-lipped niece.

'The rain's stopping,' observes my aunt, coming back into the room.

That's good.

It's Friday. I've been here three days. I like my little bedroom in the eaves, but it's a good thing I haven't brought many clothes with me. The wardrobe is tiny. There's a marble-topped washstand complete with rosy jug and basin – purely decorative – and a pretty but impractical Welsh spinning chair. The curtains are sage green, faded; one of the little square windowpanes is broken. The door has an old-fashioned latch. I like the sounds it makes.

My aunt's friend, Rosemary, bustled into the café this morning, interrupting my breakfast tea and slice of toast spread with really good local marmalade. Rosemary's blonde and plump and smells strongly of whatever it is she soaks herself in. I've adopted the seat by the inglenook fireplace, currently filled with piles of wood and knick-knacks, where I can effectively hide, quietly observing the early sunlight splashing into the tranquil café through the back window. But Rosemary soon spied me and tried to make conversation. Rosemary 'does' Saturdays, apparently, the busy period; she says she 'pops in' on other days too if there are visitors in the village, cramming into the dreary, shuttered and rambling B&B with the wrought-iron fence, or staying at the Half Moon. When she 'popped in' today, I 'popped out' gladly.

I'm walking past Mrs Fletcher's cottage on my way to the Co-op on Stile Road, a winding lane leading to a hamlet called Fall's End. It's a weird place to hide a supermarket. Mrs Fletcher's in the garden. She's thinner, older, greyer than I remember. She waves to me. I nod and quickly walk on. She's a friend of Rosemary's, and I don't want to make polite small talk just now. I really can't cope with Rosemary. She wears far too much lipstick for someone the wrong side of fifty and the chirpy chat grates on my nerves. So, when my aunt asked me to go and get some goat's milk – really? – I jumped at the chance to get out of the café and away from Rosemary's upbeat drivel.

There was another little shower overnight but today's going to be fine – according to the BBC website. I find a sliver of joy in stepping over little puddles. The May sky is a clear blue now, promising a warm day. I glance at the village hall, not far from the Co-op. That's where the village meets for jumble sales, WI meetings and – oh yes, Rosemary's 'Fellowship'. I went once, the last time I was here. I can't recall why I agreed to go.

I remember from the past, it's the only thing she talks about; I'm determined not to let her corner me with religious stuff this time around. I don't know how my aunt puts up with it. But then, she and Rosemary go 'way back', as my aunt tells me more than once, a little misty-eyed over a glass of wine in front of the telly.

I remember Rosemary's Fellowship. A couple of middle-aged women waving silky flags and a severe-faced man giving a passionate sermon about the end of the world. It's all coming back to me now. Rosemary lives in a smart bungalow in a rather exclusive cul-de-sac off the Fairleigh Road, and has a gentle, patient husband who spends a lot of time in his shed and would rather potter about in his garden than go to the Fellowship – I remember Aunty Lou saying he only turns up when there's a meeting involving some sort of food. Good man.

A sudden memory makes me chuckle. I don't know why I'd been to their place, but I was looking for Rosemary and found her husband sitting on a small chair behind the greenhouse, eating a ham sandwich. He'd looked embarrassed and I'd been bemused. Later, my aunt had told me that Rosemary didn't approve of her husband eating any sort of pork. Was that a religious thing? Poor bloke!

I push the Co-op door open. There's a tinkle. It's all bells in this village!

There's no one in there but me and the bored-looking girl on the till. I locate the milk and wonder what would happen if Tesco moved into Nun's Drift. *I bet there was a petition about the new-builds!* I browse the shelves for a while, reluctant to return to the café and Rosemary and all her relentless chat about flags or the end of the world or whatever it is she believes in.

Another tinkle. I look up and see Barny walking up to the girl on the checkout. I glance away but can't help noticing that he buys a packet of cigarettes. I think of doing the same, but I'm quitting, right?

'I'll come and sort your shelves out later,' he's saying. 'It'll be before two, but I can't say exactly when.'

'Aw, don't worry,' she replies.

'I never worry,' he answers, lightly.

'See you later, Barny.' There's more than hope in her tone.

I don't think he sees me; he's gone in an instant and I pay for the milk, noticing the girl's slightly flushed cheeks and heavily pencilled eyebrows.

I leave the shop and wander back along Stile Road. It's so quiet here, not a soul about, not even the seemingly omnipresent Barny.

There's a beep in my pocket. I feel the usual dread. Dad! He's just asking if I'm OK. But the text has unnerved me. I decide to let my feet lead me wherever they want to go.

I take a right turn rather than a left, heading away from the café, admiring the pansy-infested hanging baskets outside the flint cottages, with their neat front gardens, full of clouds of cheerful blue forget-me-nots, and red, solidly upstanding tulips. I finish up at the little lychgate, the entrance to the churchyard. Not sure how or why I'm here.

It's an imposing church, St Saviour's; solid, stoic and dependable, somehow. I know little about architecture but suddenly wish I did. The church stands proudly overlooking the village and I can't help but wonder about the stories it could tell, should it be able to speak. It also strikes me how many people are dead.

I catch my breath and survey the scene before me. Lots of graves, with half-sunken headstones; the writing is indecipherable on many of them, but one catches me. Sarah, aged twenty-six, 'dearly loved wife and mother' – she died in 1896. My age. *Micky's age.*

The grass is long in places; probably keeping it that way for the sake of nature, or maybe the church can't afford to pay someone to do too many hours per week. There are buttercups and ox-eye daisies, and soon there will be blood-red poppies and cornflowers peppering the wild grass. I remember the majestic rhododendrons in the wood behind Tony's farm. They'll be out now, although I've missed the bluebells. I feel a surge of hope, for some reason.

I don't want to leave this place just yet. I can choose the crunchy gravel path or potter through the grass; I choose the grass. It's still wet from the shower last night and the bottom of my jeans are a bit damp, but that's alright. I reach the boundary of the graveyard. I lean on the low flint wall and *breathe.* The sun is warm on my face.

I put the carton of milk down. I'm listening to a skylark soaring into the sky. The Stour Valley is spread out like a tapestry, the barley, soft green and ripening, like a vast ocean swaying in the warm breeze. *Like water.* I turn away, suddenly sickened, and find that I am not alone.

'You've got to stop following me,' he says.

'I'm not following *you*. Why are *you* following *me*?' I snap back, defensively.

Barny raises an eyebrow and nods towards a large ride-on mower, tucked away in one of the shadowy recesses of the building. 'I'm about to start work. What's your excuse?'

I hope I sound condescending. 'You do everything in this village, don't you?'

'Well, not everything.' He offers me a cigarette.

I take it – only because I'm desperate. 'I've given this up,' I say.

'Yeah, looks like it,' Barny replies, flicking a lighter. 'So, do you normally wander round graveyards on a Friday morning?'

'Just admiring the view.'

'Mmm. So am I.'

I roll my eyes, but he doesn't notice. *Typical flirt. And just a little bit dangerous.* I'm about to mention that I think I've seen him somewhere before, but he's clearly got an ego the size of this church so I don't say it. I begin to walk away.

'If you're going inside, put it out,' he calls. 'Old Dazzles doesn't like smoking in his pride and joy!'

I guess 'Old Dazzles' is a churchwarden or whatever they call them. I puff on the cigarette and a defiant cloud of smoke wafts upward. I glance over my shoulder. Barny gives a dismissive wave. I walk boldly into the porch.

Now I'm here, I might as well go in.

For all my bravado, I know I just can't smoke in the sanctuary. Why not? I lost my faith a long time ago. And now, since Micky, it's dead and buried.

I hope Micky isn't dead and buried too. *No.*

I sneak outside of the porch. I don't want Barny to see this. I stub the cigarette out. I go back inside, wondering why I care what Barny thinks.

My footsteps sound loud as I walk down the aisle. *Micky wanted to walk down the aisle.* Now I see a woman by the altar; she's twirling round, white dress, long veil, a large bunch of lilies and foliage in her hand. She's laughing.

It's not real.

I sit down on one of the cold pews, and look up at the light streaming in through the stained-glass windows: the pictures that tell a story. The one nearest me is of a shepherd holding a lamb. There's a flickering votive light on a table nearby. I find it strangely comforting.

Footsteps. Not Barny again? I glance up, but it isn't Barny. It's a man, a few years older than me, gripping a large book. He's wearing jeans but I don't miss the dog collar.

'Hello!' he says. He has kind eyes, deep brown, and they crease as he smiles. His hair is black, and his fringe flops forward almost endearingly. 'I'm Jason.' He puts his hand out so I stand and, rather awkwardly, shake it. It's a firm handshake. Suddenly, I'm really glad I put that cigarette out. 'You're Louisa's niece. From the teashop.'

News travels fast. He looks interested. I sigh. 'Meg – Meg Sperry.' Does he know? Is he going to say anything . . . ?

'Well, Meg, welcome to Nun's Drift.' Is that an Essex accent? Why did I expect him to sound middle-class vicarish? 'It's a good place.'

'Have you been here long?' I query, wondering if it sounds like a pick-up line. He clearly thinks the same and chuckles. I sit down again, feeling my face glow. He seems to take that as a cue to sit down as well. He's earnest; he leans forward, after putting his book down on the pew, and rests his elbows on his knees.

'Well, let me see. Today's Friday. That's – nine weeks and six days.' He glances at me and grins. It's a very open sort of grin.

'And that's enough time to decide it's a good place?'

'Oh yes. It's a very tight-knit community, but friendly.' He nods. 'I think there's something healing in the fabric of this place.'

'Something special and different,' I murmur.

'I'd say so.' He sits back. 'I've seen bats.'

I don't doubt it.

His eyes are wandering over the rafters; I reluctantly but with some curiosity look up too. It's like the wooden hull of a sailing ship from yesteryear. Impressive. I don't see any bats.

His voice drops almost to a whisper. 'Living here, it's like going back in time.'

'That sounds like a nightmare.'

'Why?' He doesn't look at me.

'Can't change anything.' I bite my lip, hard. 'I don't want to go back in time.'

'Sometimes you have to, for a visit. But you don't have to live there, you know.'

Those words hit me. Quietly.

It's a while before I speak again. He's watching me now.

'Not sure how long I'm going to stay.'

'In Nun's Drift? Or the past?' He half-smiles. 'If it's the past, stay just the right amount of time, Meg. Then move on.'

The stained glass is throwing rich colours onto the back of the pew in front.

'I can't move on. And I can't go back.' My heart flips over. 'I can't change anything.'

He's staring at the wooden rafters again now. 'I've got a churchyard full of dead people out there. Don't be one of them, Meg. Walk through it but don't bury yourself in it. Grief takes time.'

'What do you know about my grief?' Too quick a reply, too sharp. 'I'm sorry,' I say.

'Yours is a grief shared,' he tells me, gently.

What – my aunt has talked to the vicar about Micky? Maybe. All my family were fond of Micky – so wild, and daring, and exciting . . .

He gets up, and collects his book.

'They don't know what happened to her,' I blurt out. 'They never found a body.' Now there are tears on my cheeks. I brush them away, quickly. And I remember where I've seen Barny before. Only it isn't him.

Something about Barny reminds me of someone. Someone I knew well. Someone my best friend knew better. Someone with the same knowing eyes that I once thought crazily attractive.

There was an argument, and a car drove off leaving two broken women by a river. Shouting, crying. Micky running away. I blame myself. *Weakness.*

'Do you believe in forgiveness?' My voice is strange and hushed. I sniff, and rummage in my pocket for a tissue. 'Stupid question. It's your job, isn't it?'

'Yes, I believe in forgiveness. Sometimes we have to forgive ourselves, too. We're only human.'

I blow my nose too loudly. I smile a little, and so does he.

His footsteps fade as he heads for a side room. All is silent in the sanctuary as I dab at my eyes, and look up at the picture of the shepherd holding the lamb. The picture blurs. For a moment, I think the lamb is Micky. *She can't be dead. I won't believe it.* And it suddenly occurs to me, like a lighted candle in the darkness, just like the votive light, that either way, she's a lamb in the Shepherd's arms.

I wonder if Jason is an angel, or a ghost. It's only when I leave that I see the notices pinned on the fuzzy felt in the porch, and his name: incumbent, Rev Jason Dazely. I guess *he's* 'Old Dazzles'. I hope it's him when I hear a crunch on the gravel, but it isn't. Someone is waving a carton of goat's milk in my face.

'It'll go off in the sun,' says Barny, with his crooked smile. 'You don't want it to go sour, do you?'

I look at him. His eyes are empty. He looks as if he's carrying a burden and I wonder if he, like me, is struggling to put it down.

'You met Old Dazzles, then?' he says.

'*Old* Dazzles? He's your age.'

'Do you mind? He's older than me. Thirty-four going on sixty.'

The breeze picks up and blows my hair across my face.

'What did he think of you smoking in his precious church?' asks Barny, pleasantly, but there's an edge to his voice.

'Smoking? I've given it up,' I reply, and take the carton of milk from him. He shrugs. I'm glad to see him walk away.

I hear the mower in the distance, as I sit on the seat by the porch, with my back to the warm church wall. I hope Barny doesn't cut down the wildflowers.

I think I'll probably spend a lot of time with my back against this wall over the summer.

It's the day of the fair. I'm watching Tony drive the green traction engine into the arena and I have to laugh as the great vehicle's whistle blasts out and Tony waves to me. The *Lady Rosa*. I briefly wonder who Rosa was or is; surely it's not named after the plump woman from the Fellowship? I chuckle; no, these old engines have history . . . Then I remember Tony's partner was called Roseanne. I wonder how she's getting on with her 'fella'. A memory lodges itself in my mind: lank hair, frowning, always on her phone, trudging up the lane in green wellies, distracted, puffing on a cigarette. I'm glad I've given them up.

Anyway, Tony looks happy. The engine is such a powerful thing, and the smell of coal and oil has an olde-world comfort about it. It's a fun event, full of energy and excitement, held on what they call Church Field. I didn't know fields had names. It's accessed by a little lane that leads to Tony's farm; it runs beside the end cottage before you climb the hill to St Saviour's.

People are eating ice creams, and there are stalls full of the usual stuff that some people think is valuable; old toys, games, collectibles, reminding them of yesteryear. There are local jams, and candles made from beeswax, and woodworkers' carvings, and jewellery, and cleverly creative people keen to talk about their art. Mr Moseley's pork products are still as expensive as I remember them, and he's just as loud and overbearing. I try some of the free samples – well, you've got to, haven't you? I have to admit, the apple and honey sausage is very good.

There are a few traction engines, tractors, and cars they call 'classic'. I wander past a trio of Fords – Cortina, Zodiac, Capri – and smile at a couple of old-style Minis. The place is brim-full of nostalgia, and I suddenly notice I'm really enjoying it. It's enough to stop me in my tracks. Where did the hard-edged cynicism go?

It's a perfect day, with the sun beating down on the roofs of the vehicles, and not a cloud in the sky. I want to hold this perfect moment. Only of course, it isn't perfect. I push that thought away, but I'm not burying it. I'll look at it later.

Dad texts. I notice I'm not panicking now when he does, fearing bad news. 'Having a good time?' he writes. 'Yes!' I respond. Being in Nun's Drift has done something for me. Clever Dad. He knew it would. Suddenly, I realise I want to stay here. Who knows for how long? But helping in a café here seems a far better option than commuting to London and working in a graphic design studio overlooking the depressing backs of little terraced houses. It dawns on me. I've always felt relaxed when I'm cooking. I want to learn more. *Food hygiene training courses – need to check those online . . . Must talk to Aunty Lou . . .* I smile again. Perhaps I'm beginning, at last, to grow up.

My aunt, running the tea tent, comes out to wave at Tony as the *Lady Rosa* circles the arena. He blows her a kiss as he passes by. Her face is vivid; she looks much younger than fifty. I spot Barny, heading for the rifle range. Cornelia is tagging along behind him. She looks happy too. I hope she doesn't get hurt but I know she will. I think Tony knows that as well. I can see he doesn't like it, when he comes to the tea tent later on and Barny and Cornelia are there, her face adoring and his, impassive. Tony's expression darkens into worry. I notice Barny avoids looking at him.

Tony catches my eye briefly as he raises his mug to drink the strong brown tea. It's as if we exchange the same thought. People make choices. You can't stop them, they can only stop themselves. And if they don't, what can you do? Be there to pick up the pieces. If you can find them.

Perhaps Nun's Drift does that. Finds the pieces. Puts them back together. I have to admit, there really is something special about this place.

Micky, I'm sorry I hurt you. Maybe we'll never get the call to say you've been found. If you're alive, I hope you can forgive me. But it's been two years, Micky, two whole years, and I've spent too long in the darkness, floundering around. I need to forgive myself and move on.

Aunty Lou comes up and asks me if I'll take over from Rosemary. Rosemary's busy serving scones and tea and chatting non-stop with customers. I point out to my aunt that Rosemary seems to be doing a better job than I ever could – all I'm doing is eating the goods. But for all her steam and whistle, Rosemary means well. She catches my eye and winks at me. I smile back.

I suddenly feel the need to get away from the crowd, just for a while. I need St Saviour's and my seat by the wall. It's my sanctuary; my quiet place. My healing spot. Aunty Lou understands.

'Ten minutes,' I say.

She nods. 'Twenty, if you like.' I leave her talking to Tony, who's promising he'll be clearing those brambles tomorrow.

I walk down the lane, looking with wonder at the simplicity of the first pink wild roses scrambling in the hedge. Beautiful, and so soon over. I stop for a moment and admire them; then I walk on to the church.

I hear the traction engine's whistle again, and smile. Tony's having supper with my aunt this evening, and only I know he has something important to ask her.

There's been a wedding, and the church is full of greenery. I guess Jason has been busy. I'll be seeing him later – at the pub, for beer-battered cod and chips.

I walk up the aisle and light a votive candle.

PART TWO

Barny's Story
Not Running Away

She just won't give it a rest. If she isn't texting, she's ringing. I don't do social media and there's a reason for that. I don't want to be contacted.

I mean, I've sorted the shelves out, they've paid me. But can I go back into the Co-op? Of course not. I should never have taken her out. I only bought her a drink, for crying out loud. Now I keep getting these little heart emojis. Time to block her number.

It suddenly occurs to me: she doesn't work Thursdays or Sundays. I'll go in the Co-op when she isn't about. I could always drive to Howfield Cross; or I could go to Fairleigh – a nondescript market town, but it has a massive Tesco on the bypass. Fifteen miles, round trip. It'll be OK.

I stand up and lean against the old post. Raining again. Splashing down on the cobbles, too cold for July.

I fantasise about going somewhere warm. Spain. Hawaii. *If only!* I could spend the winter in Devon, I suppose. Got an elderly great-aunt down there who might put me up for a while. She lives in a modest apartment now, but when I was a kid, she had this draughty old house on the coast. Huge garden; I remember building lots of dens. Inside was a bit scary, though. Dark . . . strange noises . . . spooky paintings of ancestors with condemning eyes. And the bird on the landing – stuffed blackbird in a glass case. Only it wasn't black, it was white. She'd told me the story of how the other birds had drowned it in the water butt. Doesn't pay to be different, does it?

I take a last drag and drop my cigarette on the ground, grinding it into the cobbles with my heel.

There are new loose boxes opposite the old stable block. There's a clock over the entrance to the courtyard, and it'd stopped working. Jeremy Thompson-Tracey – called Jeremy by his friends, and Mr TT by me – approached me one evening in the pub and asked if I did odd jobs. Considering my van, parked right outside by the window, advertises that very fact, I decided he was just being polite. Anyway, I fixed the clock, and he was pleased. He checked it out one afternoon; he was with a slim, dark-haired girl in jodhpurs. She asked me if I'd fit some new locks on the old tack room door. It turned out she was his daughter, and she runs the riding school. I'd have thought Mr TT could have done these jobs himself, or they could have got their labourer, Ian, to do them. Still, Ian's always busy. Anyway . . . me and Mr TT get along, and he likes the occasional chat, so perhaps that's the reason I'm here. He's vague, wears baggy cords, and went to a boys' boarding school 'just out of town, in the country'. Well, you couldn't get more 'in the country' than Nun's Drift, but I think he means somewhere in Surrey. I like him, though. He looks as if he doesn't know what's going on, and he's always slightly dishevelled. *They look like that, don't they? Old money.*

I light another cigarette. Really, this rain is never going to let up. Ian's fretting. He talks about what'll happen to the corn if it gets too wet. I'm half-listening as he goes on about the wheat, waving in the breeze, dark green turning to brittle yellow, then harvest comes. He's always talking about seasons.

Maybe when I get bored of Nun's Drift, I'll try a bigger town. But I'm not bored yet.

The stable yard is shining; the sun's so bright on the wet cobbles I narrow my eyes. For a moment I almost appreciate the beauty. There's the old block I'm working in, and the new loose boxes opposite. We're a little way out of the village, on Stile Road. There are hens in the yard, and a couple of tethered goats grazing nearby. There's an overriding smell of horse, obviously. It occurs to me that I really don't mind it.

The dark-haired girl – Ally – is leading a handsome bay gelding to one of the stalls. She glances at me. I wave. She waves back.

They've got plenty of money, the Thompson-Traceys; they own most of the land around here. I'm a carpenter by trade. *Not* just an odd-job man. I'm skilled. I could have money. A place of my own. But the very thought of any kind of commitment . . . I cough.

'You want to give 'em up.'

Ian is sauntering over, hands in pockets. He's a big-boned lad in his early twenties, heavy, and a bit naïve. That's my assessment, anyway.

'That's what's makin' you cough, mate. You need to take care of yourself. You ain't a young man anymore.'

'I'm twenty-nine,' I say, pointedly.

'Old.' He shakes his head.

I finish planing the door. There, it should work OK now. I smile with satisfaction. It moves easily on the hinges. The wet has warped the wood over the years. A small job, and Mr TT didn't even ask me to do it. I must be getting soft.

Ian's forehead creases. 'I wish I was clever like you.'

I laugh. 'Clever? Yeah, so clever I'm spending all my cash on smokes and beer.'

'Aw, I don't think you drink too much, eh, Barny?'

There's something very honest about those frank blue eyes. He's right. Too many years involved in sport, knowing what I should be eating, how I should be living, has made me wiser than some. I'm about to get another cigarette out of the packet, but decide against it.

'I'm surprised they didn't get you to do all these bits and pieces,' I remark, and wonder if that was a bit insensitive. He doesn't appear to take it wrongly.

'Naw. I ain't employed by her ladyship, anyway.' He jerks his head towards the loose boxes. 'I work for her old man.' He changes the subject, deftly. 'You know that girl from the Co-op?'

'Don't think so.' I turn back to the door, thinking about my next job. Got to paint the new tack room, a really fancy upgrade from the one in the old stable block.

'She knows my sister. I think she likes you.'

I ignore that comment.

'So does Cornelia. I've seen you talkin' to her. My nan says she's a real sweetie. I thought of askin' her out myself, but then I met my missus. She's lovely, is Corny. That girl in the shop can be a bit flaky, so my sister says. You know the sort.'

I certainly do.

'And then there's this new girl. Works at the café . . . What's her name?'

'Meg.' I'm surprised I remember.

'I ain't spoken to her but she's not bad-looking with all that long, wavy hair. Nice colour. My missus says it's chestnut.' He's silent for a moment. Then he says, 'My missus says she looked *haunted* when she first arrived. Can't say I noticed.'

I don't offer my opinion.

'You know what? I reckon you could take your pick of them girls, Barny.'

'Well, so could you.'

'Naw. I'm fine with my girl. I'd never mess her around.'

'Messing around can be fun. You should try it.'

'What, and be like you? Naw.'

I don't let him see how annoyed I suddenly feel. I know he didn't mean to cause offence, and yet I *am* offended.

'You ever been married, Barny?' He's leaning against the old stone wall now, blinking in the sunshine. I wish he'd go away.

'Nope.'

'You want to get married, have kids?'

'Nope.'

'Ain't you frightened of bein' lonely when you're older?'

'I prefer to keep my options open,' I say in what I hope is the kind of tone that doesn't invite a response.

'Well, I don't. We're gettin' engaged on her birthday.'

'Big mistake. Take it from me.'

He shakes his head. 'Never gonna find another one like her, mate. She's a little diamond. And anyway – if you ain't been married, how d'you know it's a mistake?'

I take a deep breath, and then walk to my van. *Let's start the job.* He's right behind me. If I didn't think he was a bit childlike I would tell him to get lost. Yeah – I really am getting soft. I sigh as I open the back of the van: *Barny Baines, Handyman. No job too small.*

Ally walks by, slips into the old tack room, and then re-emerges with grooming gear. She walks past again, pointed chin tilted up, dark ponytail bobbing. She glances at me, and I notice she has a cute retrousse nose.

'Mornin', Miss.'

She doesn't acknowledge Ian at all.

Once she's disappeared into the loose boxes, he talks in a low voice. 'Now she's what they call *hot.*'

'I wouldn't have thought you'd notice,' I say, ironically, 'you being all loved up.'

He grins. 'Well, she's like you, ain't she? She ain't the marryin' kind, either.'

A couple of minutes later, she's striding over towards us. She's got a very determined walk. Riding boots, jodhpurs. Attractive. Someone shouts at her, gets her attention. It's one of the young girls they employ to muck out and do some grooming.

'What do you want now?' Ally's voice is shrill. I wonder how it could come from such a lovely mouth.

'Well, I've got the dentist . . .'

'What? You're always taking time off!'

The girl's face has turned red. 'I did tell you.'

Ally's face hardens. Amazing how someone can look so unattractive so quickly.

She talks to the girl in a low voice, and the girl walks away quickly, head down. What's that old story – watch how someone treats the 'little people' and you know how they'll treat you someday?

'Honestly.' Ally watches her go. 'When they say you can't get the staff, I really get what they mean.' She looks pointedly at Ian. 'Haven't you got somewhere to be?'

Ian gets the message – he's scuttling away. She turns to me. She has slate-grey eyes.

'What can I do for you?' I ask, laconically.

'Oh, quite a lot, I should imagine,' she replies.

'Well,' I nod towards the van. 'I can turn my hand to just about anything.'

'I'm sure you can. What're you doing Sunday?'

'Why, what do you have in mind?'

She's straight-faced. 'Dogs.'

'*Dogs*?'

She tells me what I'm doing Sunday. Then she disappears off to the loose boxes again, and Ian reappears, with his wide grin. I wonder where he's been hiding, listening. 'You're comin' to the gymkhana, then?'

'Looks like it.' Setting up the jumps and whatever else needs doing.

He chuckles. 'Whoever heard of a dog gymkhana, eh?'

'Yes,' I say. 'Whoever did.'

Sunday arrives, bright and warm. No sign of rain. No sign of Ian, either; he's helping get the harvest in with Tony. Yes, they help each other out, these farming types, in Nun's Drift.

I turn up at eight, as asked, and put up the last of the 'bending poles'. By ten, the meadow beside the road, half-ringed by oak trees, is crammed with people and dogs of all sorts and sizes – big, small, hairy and smooth. Judging by Ally's face, unruly behaviour won't be tolerated – by humans or animals.

Ian, Ally, Mr TT and his wife, Bella, and I set up the ring last night, and it looks pretty professional.

Bella has a mop of curly fair hair, small features and a slightly disconnected expression. With some women, you just know they were pretty when they were young. Last evening, she'd stared at me as if I was some strange insect she'd never seen before. She doesn't usually notice me; too busy making jam in her large kitchen, running the farm shop and ordering Ian's 'missus' about – poor girl works for the family part-time. I say 'poor' because the kid always looks so frightened. But I've noticed the 'little diamond's' face soften when she claps eyes on her strong, sturdy Ian, who'd never 'mess her around'.

You know, I really don't like the way Ally talks to the stable girls – and everyone else. I'd have said she was like her mother, but Ian tells me Bella isn't her mum. Bella's Mr TT's second wife, from a 'posh family', and a lot younger than him; I figure somewhere in her forties. No mention of the previous Mrs TT.

Bella swears a lot, and she did last night. She didn't like the way her husband spoke to her, and told him so. She'd stalked off, disappearing into the farmhouse at the end of the drive. Mr TT hadn't followed her, maintaining a dignified silence with a very flushed face. I had a feeling these spats happened frequently. Bella is scarily in control, and the richest man in the village just stands there and takes it.

'She won't speak to him now,' Ally confided in me, 'not for ages. He'll have to *buy* her something.' Her voice was cold. I've noticed the relationship with her stepmother. They seem to live in cool acceptance by largely ignoring each other.

Now, Ally is running about looking frazzled, barking at people, like one of the dogs. If she was a dog, I think she'd be a greyhound. Slim, elegant . . .

She barks at me: 'Barny! Can you help out in the car park? Organise the kids, alright?' She points at the field opposite, which is being used as a parking venue. I don't appreciate her tone.

I'm helping the local Scouts, not that they need any assistance. Their leader is sick, but they don't seem to need an adult to tell them what to do. A tall, pompous kid with glasses has it all wrapped up. He looks at me as if I'm an unwanted addition to the scouting fold, an irritating grown-up, so I slip off behind the stables and sit on an old tree stump there.

'Wow, Barny, that's a dangerous place to smoke. Lots of hay about. There's a sign in the yard.'

'I'm not in the yard.' I glance up, shielding my eyes from the sun's strong rays. I wonder, not for the first time, how Cornelia always seems to know where I am. She's holding a small, yappy terrier on a tight lead.

'Didn't know you had a dog,' I comment.

'Not mine. My friend's. She's ill. Something's going around. The vicar's 'ad it.'

Old Dazzles! Wondered why I hadn't seen him at this event . . . Vicars usually like to mingle with their flock, don't they?

'We're entered in the Small Dog Jumping,' she's saying.

'Have fun.' The terrier's sniffing at my feet. I stand up, and step away.

'You're not keen on dogs, then?'

'You've noticed.'

'Where d'you come from?' she asks, all of a sudden. She seats herself on the tree stump. 'You never say. Where were you born? You're a right mystery, like.'

'Am I?'

'Aw, c'mon. I'm your friend! Let me in on the secret.'

I've talked to her a bit, and bought her a cup of tea at the summer fair. Does that make us friends? *Like women who think you're in a relationship, just because you sleep with them* . . . My gut twists at a sudden memory.

'It's not a secret.' The irritation comes out in my voice and she looks hurt. I run a hand through my hair. 'Kent —

Rochester.' I name my moves one by one. As I reel them off, the words seem to turn to ashes in my mouth.

I'm actually relieved to see Ally appear around the side of the building. I drop my cigarette and crush it into the dirt.

'I hope you weren't smoking,' says Ally.

'I hope you weren't watching,' I reply.

'Hello, Cornelia.' I'm interested to see the thinly veiled dislike in her face. 'Have you registered your dog? In the farm shop . . .'

'Yes.' Cornelia's answer is curt. No love lost between these two, clearly.

'Barny, can I borrow you?' Ally comes up to me, links her arm in mine, and tries to steer me away.

I don't think I want to be *borrowed* by this woman.

I turn and wink at Cornelia. 'See you later, yeah?'

Ally's seen the wink.

Good.

She wants me to help in the shop. Bella – who has been registering dogs – has decided she's had enough for the day; she wants to be with friends, and enjoy the show. Ian's missus usually helps but she isn't well – another one with whatever's 'going around'. I'm beginning to think I'm being opted onto Ally's personal service squad. Perhaps I *am* her personal service squad.

I recognise a woman, browsing, a canvas bag over her shoulder. I think about what Ian's missus said about her. Haunted? I thought she was just moody. Cornelia's mentioned there was a problem in the past, but she won't say what, and I haven't pushed it. Not interested enough. As I watch her bend over the organic veg, though, I frown. She's put some weight on. It suits her. She was too skinny when she first arrived.

'Hello,' I say.

Meg turns and looks at me, surprised.

'Oh, hi,' she says, a bit dismissively. 'Didn't know you worked here.'

'I didn't know it, either!' I lean back on the counter, folding my arms.

'You really are everywhere, aren't you?'

'You following my every move? I'm flattered.' No response. I clear my throat. 'New career prospects. Who knows, I might get used to it. Selling organic carrots could be a new, good and wholesome career change for me. And I'll be able to see in the dark.'

Now she can't hide a smile. I notice it softens her face.

'Well, Nun's Drift opens up a whole new world, doesn't it?' she says.

'Does it?'

'Well, it has for me. There you go.'

'You've given up smoking, then?'

'Definitely. You?'

'You've got be joking. Got to have some pleasure in life.'

She doesn't answer.

I remember the last time I saw her – it was a couple of weeks ago, in the graveyard, sitting outside the church. Old Dazzles, the vicar, was talking to me about doing some work in the church hall. I was working out when I could fit it in. I remember Dazzles saying hello to her. It was a warm hello.

She puts carrots and celery on the counter. 'I think you're meant to be on the other side of it,' she points out. 'The till side.'

I'm close enough to see her eyes are green. Never noticed before. I stand up straight, go round the other side of the counter, and take her money. I put the veg in a paper bag, and hand it to her.

'Service with a smile, eh?' she comments, drily, but I notice her eyes twinkle.

'Always.' I watch her leave the shop.

Ian appears, just when the show's over and everything's done. I've just arrived back at my van, longing for a sandwich, a pint and a smoke.

'How did it go, then?'

'Someone's sheepdog won just about everything,' I tell him. 'Get all the wheat in?'

'Yep. Tony's happy.' He laughs a bit. 'I'll get you right trained up yet . . . tellin' the difference between wheat and barley.' His forehead creases. 'You workin' 'ere again this week?'

'Yep. Painting the new office.'

'Barny!' Ally's voice, crisp and demanding, is behind us. 'Can I have a word?'

Ian gives me a knowing look, mutters something about seeing his missus, and lopes away. I avoid Ally's very direct gaze.

'Can I just see that cream paint – the topcoat we agreed?'

'Yep, I'll get it tomorrow.' I reach into my pocket and get my phone. I move close to her as I show her the picture.

'Oh yes, right.' She sounds breathless. She slips her hair out of the ponytail and lets it lie loose around her shoulders. It isn't that long, and very straight. She makes quite a fuss of tying it back again. Pocketing the phone, I lean back against the van and fold my arms, observing her. She notices.

Just after lunch, Friday. I'm sitting in the van having my sandwiches, window down, radio softly playing. A bunch of kids on ponies are having a great time in a nearby paddock full of cavaletti. A woman is standing by the fence, laughing fondly at a small child on a grey mare, attempting the jumps: 'Well done, darling! Show her who's boss!'

I switch the radio off. Time to think. This job's kept me going for a while, and I've got other work lined up in the village next week – start of August. Still not bored with Nun's Drift. This village has 'got something' – what? Don't know. Can't define it. Just a nice feel.

I'm startled when someone appears at my window.

'Barny!' Ally nods towards the old office. 'Can you just ...' She raises a well-plucked eyebrow.

'Got to make a call, OK?' I wave my phone in her face and I notice a surprised expression.

'Oh – well ...'

'Five minutes,' I say.

'Alright.'

She doesn't look pleased. She walks into the old office. I wonder who will help her shift all the stuff into the new space. It won't be me. I put the phone on the passenger seat and eat the rest of my sandwich. I hope she's watching.

Ten minutes later, I get out of the van and slam the door. It's ancient, that van, but it does the trick. Be great to buy a new one, though. I glance at the Range Rover in the yard, the Audi, and Ally's brand-new Mini.

I stroll leisurely to the office, and push open the door. The swivel chair turns. *Hmm. She's got be to be thirty at least* . . .

'Is everything OK?' I say, lightly. I'm suddenly aware of paint covering my jeans and T-shirt. Ally looks immaculate – I wonder how she does that, working with horses. Nice face, nice body. And she knows it. She's let her hair down again.

'Well, yes. The tack room looks good, and the new office is looking smart,' she says, picking up a pen and jiggling it between two fingers.

'You'll have my invoice, then.' I turn to go.

'Oh, that's not what I want to talk to you about.' The sun's coming through the poky window, and I notice a web in the corner of the room. No sign of a spider but I know it's there.

'I just wondered if you'd be available to . . . well, if you want more.' I turn and face her. After too long a pause she adds, 'More work.'

I put my hands on my hips and smile. She smiles back, standing up, tossing her hair in the way girls do.

I shake my head. 'I don't think so.'

'What?' A little frown appears between the grey eyes.

'Nah, I have other . . . work.'

'Oh. So you're not interested in . . .'

'No,' I say, with another smile. 'Thanks for the offer, though.'

I wink at her, and walk out. I feel good about that. I can't stand these girls who think they're something.

I'm standing at the bar at the Half Moon. Louisa and Tony are there tonight, laughing in the corner, by the window. They're getting married soon – February, I think someone said. Everyone's at it. Commitment!

I turn back to the bar and have a weird moment where I'm looking at myself. There's a mirror opposite me, and I see a fella with fair hair staring back. Good-looking, yes. Getting older, yes. If I didn't know him, I'd say he looks jaded. I'd rather stare at my drink.

I like the Half Moon. The owner's a nice guy, cheerful and friendly. I hear my name being called. Tony's beckoning me over. I'm surprised. He's in here a lot, and he doesn't usually talk to me. I always get the feeling he's sizing me up and doesn't much like what he sees. I tend to avoid him, if I can. But he's really happy tonight – about the harvest, I guess.

'C'mon, Barny, don't be on your own, you miserable bloke. Come and sit with us.'

Louisa shifts along a little as I sit down on the cushioned bench. She puts her hand on my arm. A shock runs through me. Something about her in that moment reminds me of my mum. I breathe in, sharply.

'You OK?' she asks, concerned.

'Everyone's getting married!' laughs Tony, suddenly. 'Ian up at Jeremy's farm, he's talking about getting wed next summer. I remember him as a little lad. We're all getting older, Barny. Life's moving on. What about you, eh? You're a part of the community now. Get yourself a nice lady, and settle down. Eh?' He leans across the table, and there's a glint in his eye. 'As long as it isn't my Corny.'

'Tony!' exclaims Louisa.

'Nope. Not Cornelia.' I put my hand up. 'Just friends.'

Tony scrutinises my face and then sits back, apparently satisfied with my answer. *Good. Don't want any trouble here.*

'Anyway,' I add, 'I'm a rolling stone. Always moving on.'

'Can't run forever, mate,' he says, bluntly.

Run? Who said I'm running? I stare at him. He doesn't notice, but Louisa does. She moves uneasily next to me, and looks at him in a warning kind of way.

Moving on. Yep. That's my game. But not quite yet. I take a sip of my beer as the door slams open and a group of twenty-somethings walk in. I see Ally among them, with some fella's arm around her. He's dark, fit – and looks younger than her. I guess she's got a point to prove. She glares at me. I pretend I haven't noticed. She tosses her hair, talking loudly.

Two horses trot by the window, the riders laughing and carefree. Ally is braying like a donkey. I drain my glass.

'You're a good man.' Louisa squeezes my arm. I wish she wouldn't. 'It's a lovely evening,' she continues, letting go and looking out of the small-paned glass. 'We should go for a walk, Tony, down by the river. Come on! It'll do you good.'

Do him good? Well, maybe it will sober him up.

'Yeah. Why not?' He looks at me. 'C'mon, Barny, you come too. You don't want to be stuck in here with *that* lot, do you?'

The young men are braying now.

'Well . . .'

'Aw, come on,' says Tony, rising, and hauling me to my feet. 'Be sociable. You're not such a bad lad.'

I'm relieved that's his opinion – even if it's just the drink talking. The three of us leave, and I take a deep breath. The evening air is warm and muggy.

'Good job we got that field done,' mutters Tony. 'There's a storm coming.'

Louisa links her arm with mine. I politely unhook her. Too unwelcome. Too many memories.

'You two enjoy yourselves. Don't let him fall in the river, Louisa – he's had a skinful.'

'You cheeky—' Tony laughs and gives me a bear hug all of a sudden. He smells of beer. And there I am again, a young boy, hugged by my dad, both of us lost and crying.

I can't speak now. I go and sit under the horse chestnut tree, on the circular seat. Circular; round and round, like life. I shift so I sit on the other side, facing away from the pub.

My mind flips and I can see my mum. I don't want to see her. My hand is shaking slightly as I light my cigarette.

'Penny for 'em?'

Cornelia's voice cuts through the fog of unwanted memories. How long have I been sitting here? It's getting dark.

She sits next to me. She's fragrant – a light, flowery scent.

'Oh, just thinking about my next job,' I lie.

She's wearing a long, floral skirt; pretty in the twilight. Ian's nan is right. She *is* a sweetie. I can almost see two kids, and Cornelia baking in a small kitchen, flour on her nose. It's a strange thought, and not one I've ever entertained before. For a moment I feel disorientated.

'I miss talkin' to you, you know,' she says. 'You've been so busy at the stables, I've 'ardly seen you.'

This girl is see-through. No guile.

'Well,' I say. 'I've got to work.' I stub my cigarette out, stand up, and stretch.

She stands up, too. 'Let's go for a walk. By the river, maybe?'

I look down at her eager face. It'd be so easy . . .

'Nah. There's a storm coming . . . so they say. Your uncle's down there, anyway, with Louisa.'

Her face falls. 'Barny – can I ask you something, like?'

Please, please don't ask me if we can go on a date.

'Are you going to stay in Nun's Drift? You never told me why you came 'ere in the first place.'

No, I didn't.

'You never stay anywhere very long and you've told me you've moved around a lot. Billericay, Dunmow, Coggeshall, a place on the Blackwater, Colchester, Stowmarket, Sudbury. You spent six months in Felixstowe and you were born in Rochester.' She looks delighted to have remembered it all, and I'm a bit disturbed that she has. She moves towards me. I take a step back. 'I don't want you to leave, Barny, I really don't. I like talkin' to you. I wish we could talk more, you know.'

I look at her, wondering if anyone has ever kissed her.

'Well,' I say. 'I'm not feeling very talkative tonight. Too tired. I'm going home.' I correct myself. 'Mrs F's – Mrs Fletcher's.'

'Oh, such a beautiful cottage, ain't it, with all them hollyhocks and California poppies out front, and sunflowers? Her 'usband used to grow the best chrysanthemums in the village, they say. I'd love to live in a cottage like that.'

'Well, maybe someday you will.'

She tilts her head to one side. 'You reckon?'

Yeah . . . but not with me. I walk away.

And now, I wonder if I should be moving on from Nun's Drift.

In bed that night, rain lashing the little windows, I find I can't stop thinking about Cornelia. Then I think about Ally. Then I think about Meg.

I get up feeling wrecked. Mrs F has gone off to some Saturday morning meeting – she does stuff for the church, as well as what she calls 'chores' for Old Dazzles. She's alright, is Mrs F – not like that nosy old bat Rosemary, who always looks at me as if she disapproves of my very existence. Mrs F treats me more like a family member than a paying guest. She's a widow – lonely, I suppose.

She's left a note by the cereal boxes in the dining room. There's some 'proper breakfast' in the kitchen, and could I have a quick look at that cupboard under the sink, the one with the dodgy door?

I go into the kitchen and stare at the eggs, waiting in the pan, inviting me to light the gas, boil them and be sensible.

I yawn and light a cigarette instead. Then I move into the garden, knowing how much Mrs F hates the smell of smoke indoors.

Nothing much to do today. I decide to just chill out. I know that annoying girl isn't working in the Co-op today because someone said she's ill. So that's good news. I can nip in there and get some smokes.

Nice morning, wet pavements, after the storm last night. Maybe *that's* what disturbed my sleep. But before I can get to the shop, I hear something. Raised voices. Two women. *Uh-oh.*

'He's not *yours*, you silly little girl!'

'Well, 'e ain't yours, either!'

'You need to grow up! I could tell you a thing or two.' Ally lowers her voice, and I can't hear what she's saying. I see Cornelia's reaction, though. Ally's finished. She goes to her Mini, parked outside the Co-op, gets in and slams the door. She speeds off. Then Cornelia sees me.

'Barny!' She half-runs over. There are tears on her cheeks. 'Is it true? You ain't really after Ally, are you?'

What?

She tries to embrace me, but I hold her at arm's length. She starts to properly cry. I freeze; I don't even try to deny it. I turn away. She's just a kid with a crush. And an uncle with an attitude, a drink problem – and a shotgun.

Decision made. It's getting too difficult here, just like it does everywhere. I'm packing my bags. My phone's on the bed, switched off. *Yeah, Tony, I'm running away . . . again.*

I look out of the little low window in my bedroom. I can see the village green, empty of dog walkers and children and people talking that Sunday morning. Maybe they're all in church. Church! I promised Old Dazzles I'd do some work for him in September. Could I just leave and not let him know? I'm tempted.

I sit down on the bed and sigh. Many of the jobs I've had in the village have come via Dazzles – Jason. People have told me that 'the vicar said' I'm reliable. I've done some work in the vicarage, and I take care of the churchyard – cut the grass and all that. Reluctantly, I admit he's been good to me, has Dazzles. But he's been ill. Will he even be at the church, if I wait outside for him? I look at my mobile, lying on the bed beside me. Could ring him, I think, unenthusiastically, or send a message. But I don't want to switch it on. *No hassle.*

I'm sitting on the bench by the porch as the parishioners leave. My back's to the old flint wall and the sun's beating down on the dusty, dark trees beyond the churchyard. The parishioners are chattering; a few of them notice me and say hello, but for the most part they're getting on with their lives, ambling home for Sunday lunch. Time seems to stand still in Nun's Drift.

The last of them gone, I stand up. Beautiful view over Tony's fields, with the cut corn in the distance, coarse yellow stubble waiting to be ploughed; I watch a couple of horses cantering across them, riders leaning forward.

Seasons. I take a last puff of my cigarette, drop it, and grind the butt into the gravel.

Footsteps. Someone's coming out. I recognise Dazzles' voice and I'm relieved. I don't really want to go into the church. I don't do churches; too creepy, reminds me of death.

The vicar's standing there, surprised to see me. He's a bit gaunt; looks like he's been properly sick.

He's not alone. The chestnut-haired girl with him looks surprised too.

'Hi, Barny,' she says.

'Hello.' I feel uncharacteristically awkward.

'Coming to church?' There's that twinkle in her eyes. 'You're a bit late for the service.'

'I'm not,' I say, too quickly. 'Not coming to – look, I want a word with Da – Jason.'

'Oh, right.' She twinkles again. For a moment I think she's enjoying my discomfort. 'I'll see you tomorrow, then,' she says to Dazzles, and he nods.

What does she mean, she'll see him tomorrow?

I didn't know she was into church. Seen her sitting outside it when I've been cutting the grass – on the very seat I've just got up from. But she goes to services too?

'How can I help you, Barny? I'm so sorry – I've not been well. I was meaning to talk to you about the church hall.'

I tear my gaze away from Meg, walking down the path between the gravestones.

'Oh, yeah. OK.' I turn my attention to the vicar. 'Well, here's the thing. I'm moving on.'

He's got an intense face. I've never really noticed it before. I've always thought he was way older than his years, like an old man in a young body, and I suppose I've found that funny. But right now, I know it isn't, really.

He's blinking at me as he gives me coffee in a fancy mug with a poppy on it. I expected some religious slogan, not 'Be Fabulous'. I have absolutely no time for religion. My dad's always quoting the Bible – in-between getting drunk and getting emotional.

I'm sitting on a squashy sofa that's seen better days. The vicarage, with its sweeping drive, opposite the church, is enormous. One fella living in it. I can't help but feel annoyed about that. *He gets it free, doesn't he? And what does he do for a living? Preaches, holds old ladies' hands . . . and chats up young women?* Still, he's always been alright with me. I feel ever so slightly ashamed I've always called him Old Dazzles, had a crafty laugh at him – he just seemed so 'proper', somehow, old-fashioned, quirky, odd. When I worked in the vicarage, he was clearly wary, but friendly. I'd painted one of the bedrooms; there'd been a leak and it was a mess. He'd talked about bats in the church tower and how fascinating they were. I'd thought (but not said) he needed to get out more.

'So Barny,' he says, now, 'you're moving on again. I remember you telling me you'd been about a bit.'

That's a fact.

He sits down on a hard-backed chair that's a bit creaky. He clears some papers, an open bag of liquorice allsorts and other junk away from the cluttered desk and places his mug down on a tea-stained coaster.

'I've had this bug that's going round,' he says, pulling a face.

'Ah well, I suppose you vicars get well looked after.' *Oops. Shouldn't have said that.*

Fortunately, he laughs. 'People always seem to think we have an easy life. Working one day a week and all that sort of thing. Living in some idyllic place like Nun's Drift in a big house.'

'Well . . . if the cap fits.'

He shakes his head. 'It's a long way from where it all started. Where did it start for you, Barny?'

Why do you want to know?

I say, grudgingly, 'Rochester.'

'Kent! Ah, I was just over the water from you. Near Southend.'

He's an Essex boy! I smile.

'Why do you want to move on?' He's leaning forward, interested.

I don't want to tell him – I never tell anyone when I leave.

'Things just get complicated sometimes.' I shrug. 'That's all. Time to go.'

He seems to be thinking. Then he says, quietly, 'It's a pattern, isn't it?'

'What?'

He reaches for his mug, and studies the contents. There's a loud-ticking grandfather clock in the hall, just outside the study door, which is ajar. A tabby cat strolls in, rubs itself against Jason's knees, and stares at me with some disdain before wandering out. It reminds me of Ally.

'Well, it's alright for you,' I say, and the sharpness of my tone shocks me. 'I bet you've had it easy. I haven't. I've got to keep moving.'

He nods. 'We all have our escapes, Barny. Mine used to be martial arts. For some of my friends, it was drinking, drugs.'

I find it very hard indeed to imagine Old Dazzles as some sort of ninja, and I almost spill my coffee in surprise.

'What did *you* need to escape from?' It comes out too harshly. He takes a moment, then tells me a story of a man who beat up his girlfriend's son on a regular basis. So, when the boy was older, he learned how to handle himself. The guy left, but the boy was still angry. He carried it for a long time. He still gets nightmares, but not so many these days.

He stops talking and lowers his eyes. The clock ticks. The cat reappears, looks around, and settles on a chair by the Georgian window.

I put the mug down on the small table in front of me, breaking the silence.

'You ever seen that film *Shane*?'

'Oh, that was a book too, wasn't it?' He looks up. 'The gunfighter who's trying to run from his past . . . and can't.'

'Well, I'm like that. I move on because – well, trouble follows me.' I realise how ridiculously dramatic that sounds. I feel embarrassed and shift uneasily in my seat. 'Oh, and before you ask, I'm not in *that* kind of trouble. With the law, I mean.'

'There are different types of trouble, Barny, you and I both know that. Unfortunately, we tend to carry our past with us. We can't outrun it.'

I feel deflated. 'You're saying wherever I go, it'll follow me. Always affect me. I'll always be running.'

'No. I'm just saying it takes a lot of guts to stand and face it.'

I run my hand through my hair. 'I can't.'

'You have to put the old stuff down, take a good long look at it, and deal with it. You *can* move on, but you need to do it *in here.*' Jason taps his chest.

'I can't.' Suddenly I blurt it out. 'You don't understand. I just go from woman to woman. I don't even *like* most of them. Every time, it all goes wrong, there's tears, there's trouble, and I can't handle it. So, I move on.' There's a heavy weight on my chest. 'When I came here, I tried to stay away from them. But I can't. I just can't do it . . . I don't want to be that way, but . . .' I can't breathe and my thoughts are disjointed and jumbled. 'My mum. She had an affair . . . My dad fell apart.' My voice is hoarse. 'I just can't *trust* anyone!'

He's got his arm round my shoulder. And now I'm weeping.

I haven't cried since I was eleven, and Mum walked out.

Later, I leave the vicarage and stand for a moment in the afternoon sun. Instead of turning left at the end of the drive, I cross the road, heading for the churchyard. Jason talked about faith, about healing, about restoration. Lots of words that mean little to me. He prayed. Nothing religious, just a few words that I can't remember. I'm shaken, but I've started to feel the first glimmer of hope that maybe life *can* be different.

He says there are other men who've got stories to tell, and would I like to meet them? They're gathering tonight in someone's house in Fairleigh for snacks and a chat. Nothing heavy. I don't know. What did Jason say? One day at a time? So much to process.

I wander into the churchyard and look at the gravestones. *Life's short. Even if you live to be eighty years old, it's still so brief.* I sit on my favourite seat, by the porch. For some reason, I think of Meg. Of course, it's the seat she seems to like too.

I want to live before I die. Live well. Is it actually possible? Can I really have a life where I don't have to keep running? I think of the packed suitcase in my bedroom. *Seasons.* That word comes to mind again. Maybe it means something. Maybe it doesn't.

Shall I take a chance and go to that meeting tonight, with Jason?

A car goes past on the hill, breaking my solitude. I need to go back to my lodgings.

Back at Mrs F's, there's a note on the kitchen table. My dinner's in the oven. I remember how she likes to cook me a 'proper meal' on Sundays. She hopes it isn't ruined. But there's no 'telling off' in that note, and even for that small kindness, I'm grateful.

Before I eat, I take the stairs two at a time and grab my phone from the bed. Decision made. I ignore all the messages and, taking a deep breath, send just one.

PART THREE

Rosemary's Story
Doubt

It's not just me. Everyone says it. She's *lighter*.

I bring the tray out of the oven. *That'll* bring him in. He can smell my cakes from the bottom of our eighty-foot garden. Oh yes. My cakes are well known in the village.

As I scoop them off the tray onto the wire to cool, I find myself thinking about Meg again. Megan – that's her real name. She's changed since she came to Nun's Drift. She always avoided speaking to me, even when she lived here before, and I must say I thought she was a troubled girl. But now she's working at the café, and she's done her food hygiene course, and she wanted to learn to bake. I agreed to teach her. So . . . we're not quite friends, but we've shared a few jokes lately, over the cream teas.

I go to the window and see him, engrossed in clearing something out of a big container. I tap my nails on the glass and mouth, 'Cakes! Are you coming in?' and he nods, wiping his mucky hands on his trousers. I inwardly groan. *Oh, don't do that...*

Of course, he spends a lot of time in his shed. Arthur's a wonderful man, very interested in his garden. He's in the utility room, and then pads into the kitchen, plonking himself down at our rather nice pine table. It matches the pine dresser.

'Oh, Arthur! The state of those socks.' I put a plate in front of him. A lovely pattern – old roses.

'I like them,' he says. His hair's thinning. I wonder where my handsome beau of years past has gone. But then, I'm no longer the slim and attractive woman he married.

'How's that lawnmower?' I pour him a cup of tea – not too weak, not too strong.

'It's *broken*, Rose. I'll take it to the tip.'

Do I detect a hint of annoyance?

I'd prayed for it. I'd laid hands on it and commanded it to work in the name of the good Lord, just like the pastor told me. Arthur said the motor's gone. Well, I'd said, the good Lord can bring it back. Arthur had rolled his eyes, and went out and bought a Flymo.

I'm sitting in the little Fellowship. Our meetings are held in the old village hall, and we look out onto the Thompson-Traceys' vast tracts of land. This place is ancient, it's crumbling, it smells of damp and no one really uses it anymore except for the odd jumble sale. Even the WI have abandoned it. They're all using the big church hall now – nice and new with good lavatories. It's always so *cold* in here. It'd seem a bit cheeky to ask the vicar if we could use the church hall, but I do wish we could find somewhere warmer.

I find my eyes wandering from the stark, bare walls to the tractor, ploughing the field that runs beside the building. The earth is being turned, and underneath, it's a rich brown. All the dry, dead stubble is gone; all that's left, row after row, is the fresh earth. I can smell it through the open window. It's open because it's broken . . .

A thought pops into my head. My life feels just like that earth. I feel as if I'm being churned up. Ploughing goes deep. What's buried is brought to the surface.

A sudden shaft of sunlight makes me squint. It's as if God is pointing his heavenly finger at me.

I try to bring myself back to the present moment. Bless him, Gordon is still talking. What's he on about? Oh yes, the end of the world – again. Oh, I do *wish* he had a less sonorous voice. I glance at the other members of the congregation. My notebook is on my knee. I start to scribble, as if I'm listening to the sermon. I try to look engaged in what he's saying. But I'm not. My scribblings are, in fact, a shopping list. Sourdough, crème fraiche, chicken breast (x2). Must get that from Moseley. I wonder if the farm shop is open on Sundays. I suppose it is. It feels a bit naughty to think about slipping along there after church. I never shop on Sundays. I suddenly quite fancy getting some of his speciality sausages. But I can't. The Fellowship doesn't approve of pork products.

I glance sideways as someone coughs. Only four in the congregation today, plus me. It's been dwindling. I blame the internet – and the village football team. They play on

Sundays and lots of the younger people are involved with that. Then there's the DIY store in Fairleigh; people flock there. And the garden centre ...

There's Mrs Fordham, hunched over in her usual place. She's nearly ninety. And Paula Bellwood, late thirties, never married, very intelligent, very serious. Her mother runs *Bellwood's Antiques* in the village; they live together, but they don't get on.

In the front, there's the old chap who lives next door to the pub. He never says anything. Mr Silent, I call him. Sitting beside me is Anne, the pastor's wife. She's looking at me now. I smile. She doesn't smile back. I turn my attention to her husband, and hope more frantic scribbling gets me back in her good books. She wasn't very pleased this morning when I forgot the flags.

I always bring the flags. Two of them, one gold, one white. They symbolise something, but I can't remember what, and today I really don't care. I used to love my flags, waving them in worship as earnestly as I could. Nearly took someone's head off once. But now I wonder why I bothered making them.

'The notices ...'

Oh! He's finished. I start thinking about those sausages again. I sigh. I can't get the sausages. But I *can* get the chicken breasts.

Gordon glares at us from the front. He's gripping his big Bible — King James Version, he never uses anything else. *Shakespearean English.* Hmm. I used to like Shakespeare, at school. *A Midsummer Night's Dream;* not sure Anne and Gordon would approve ...

'The council are closing the hall!'

It's announced as if it's the worst thing that ever happened in the history of humankind. I want to shout 'Hallelujah!' but I suppose that wouldn't be right. I rummage in my bag for a mint.

'We need to pray!' he says, very loudly. I look up. He waves the Bible in our general direction. 'This is an opportunity for *much* larger premises. We shall sow in faith! A bigger building! Yes! And then the people will come.'

I feel like adding, 'Not if you haven't got heating, they won't!' But Mrs Fordham speaks. She has a surprisingly strong voice for one so elderly – very clipped. 'Why don't we just ask that nice vicar if we could borrow the church hall?'

Gordon looks aghast. 'The *Church of England* hall?' Oh no. We're going to get a lecture now. I groan, but turn it into a cough.

'I'm very surprised, Rosemary,' says Anne, later, as we're drinking weak tea from little chipped cups, 'that you forgot the flags today.'

'I'm sorry, Anne. I can't imagine what came over me.' I'm wondering how I can slip off to the farm shop without her seeing. I put my cup down.

Anne stares at me out of very round eyes. They narrow slightly. She must be younger than me, but not by many years. We're friends, but she's never admitted her age. She never wears make-up, either, and at that moment I think she could do with some foundation to even out her skin tone. Then I have a terrible thought. I look down at my cup. Red marks on the rim give the game away. I always remember to not wear lipstick when I go to church. Until today.

I quickly put my thumb over the mark, rubbing the rim quickly. Too late. I know she's seen it.

'Rosemary,' she says, carefully, 'is everything alright at home?'

'Oh yes! Why?'

'We've been praying for Arthur this week. Has he shown any signs of—'

'He doesn't want to come to church, no.' I'm still rubbing the rim. I feel suddenly nervous.

Mrs Fordham's granddaughter has turned up. 'Come on, Nan,' she says, in a bored voice. She turns to go, and Mrs Fordham trots behind her, dutifully.

'Mrs Fordham! Can we have a little chat?' Anne calls to her, but the granddaughter, a lanky girl with several facial piercings, answers before the old lady can respond.

'I've got to get her home, OK? She can talk to you later, alright?'

Anne doesn't reply. She grips my arm, then, and her fingers are like little sticks. She leans so close I find myself automatically leaning backwards.

'Rosemary! I feel the Lord saying, "Don't start slipping and sliding." Be very careful.'

'Slipping and sliding?' I try to laugh it off. 'I really must buy some sensible shoes!'

She says nothing. I'm chastened.

Honestly, I feel like one of those SAS people. I'm hiding behind a tree, for goodness' sake. I shouldn't have to do this at my age. I'm – well, I'll admit to 'fifties'.

Anne and Gordon are at our bungalow. They're ringing the rather splendid bell that Arthur installed. He isn't answering. He never answers the door to them – ever. I shrink closer to the tree, holding my breath as they put something through the letter box and get back into their old Corsa. They drive off. I breathe out. The chicken breasts are safe in the bag, if a bit squashed.

I make a dash for it, up the driveway – Arthur has weeded it, very nice – and in through the front door as quickly as I can.

I lean against the wall, panting.

'Good gracious!' My husband starts as he comes out of the living room, holding his newspaper. He does love his old-fashioned papers. 'Are you alright?'

'Fine!' I scurry into the kitchen.

'Your lot were just here. They left this.' He hands me a leaflet. I put it on the pine table and wipe my hand over my face. I feel like I've been on manoeuvres, or whatever it is the army does.

'What's that, Rose? Chicken?'

'Yes. From the farm shop.'

He stares in surprise. I can see what he's thinking: *Shopping on a Sunday?* But he doesn't say it. He bites his lip, then mumbles, 'I'd quite like some of their sausages, you know.'

'Well, you can't have them!' I snap. 'Or bacon. Or ham.'

'Alright, Rose.' He sighs. 'I suppose lunch will be a bit late, then. Think I'll wander off to the shed.'

He does, and I'm relieved, if a little vexed. He's *always* in that shed. I used to wonder what he did in there, but I peered through the window once, so I know. He reads

Gardening Tips Monthly. He never seems to read any of the Bible tracts I leave around the house in strategic places.

I mean, I have. I've left them everywhere. In the kitchen, in the living room, in the dining room, in the bedroom, in the loo. He should be the most avid churchgoer by now. Good grief, he should be a pastor. Actually, I've been leaving those tracts everywhere *for years*. Most people are polite about it. Some aren't. That arrogant Thompson-Tracey girl from the farm was the rudest of all. She'd once shouted at me that I was a God-botherer. But then, I had just put a tract through her car's open window while she was waiting at the T-junction by the B&B.

I suddenly feel a great surge of anger. I put the paprika-covered chicken breasts in some foil, and slam them into the fan oven. I put some potatoes, broccoli and carrots in the steamer. Then I go through the whole house and pick up every wretched leaflet I've ever left anywhere. I mean, I *dust around them.* And dusty they are, too.

I've got a pile in my hand and I have an idea. I don't hesitate. I shove them in the recycling sack. It's very satisfying.

'Are you alright, Rose?' Arthur says, popping his head round the kitchen door. 'Didn't mean to upset you or anything.'

'I'm absolutely wonderfully fine,' I reply, firmly.

'Oh – well, jolly good.'

'Fancy a cuppa?'

He nods, and disappears back to the shed.

One leaflet is left on the table, I notice. It's the one Anne dropped off earlier – the one Gordon has written himself and got printed. All bold capital letters, exclamation marks and warnings. The anger surges over me again. 'Oh, shut up!' I say, out loud, tossing the tract in the bin.

Next Sunday morning, I'm not in church. I'm in the spare bedroom, looking through old photo albums. I've been busy this week. Most people spring-clean, but I do a thorough turnout every autumn. The leaves are falling; Arthur's trying to catch them in the vacuum-like thing he's bought, before it rains. I actually feel quite comfortable, alone in that room.

I smile as I see my schoolfriends, fresh-faced, not knowing what was to come. What did I think my life would be, when I was fourteen? I look up, absently, at the very pretty lemon curtains. They match the duvet cover. Of course.

All I wanted when I was fourteen was a nice job, and then a family. I used to discuss it with my best friend, Lizzy. She laughed and said she just wanted horses. She got them, of course – she married a *very* wealthy man. I remember the night she met him. We were at a Young Farmers dance, and he was standing by the door looking tall, rich and awkward. All the girls were fawning over him, but Lizzy just started dancing on her own. He couldn't take his eyes off her. So, she got her horses, and eventually she had a baby too.

Lizzy was my only bridesmaid when I married Arthur. I smile a little at the memory. He was older than me, an accountant, very quiet. I was in my thirties. I loved my job as a secretary, but I wanted so badly to meet the right man and have a family. I remember how scared I'd been that I was leaving it too late. When would Mr Right turn up? It was the first time I prayed. 'Oh God! Please, let me meet the right man *soon.*'

I look at my happy little fourteen-year-old face, so full of life and hope. I feel sudden tears pricking my eyelids. They do that quite a lot these days. *If only we could have had children.*

This won't do. I put the photo albums aside, get up, and face the door. There are the flags, leaning against the chest of drawers.

I've been a believer for years now. Used to go along to the Baptist church in Fairleigh. Then I met Anne and Gordon, and they told me lots of things I didn't know about the Bible. Hence the tracts everywhere, trying to get Arthur interested. And laying hands on the lawnmower.

Well, that didn't work, did it?

I'm wiping the windows over when someone rings the bell. Without checking – we have this wonderful little spyhole Arthur put in place – I open the door. If I was feeling troubled before, I feel worse now.

'Rosemary! So glad I've caught you . . .'

'Oh, hello, Anne.' I'm aware I'm holding a damp cloth in my hand, and find myself twisting it nervously between my fingers.

'Missed you yesterday at the Fellowship. And last Tuesday, at the Bible study. We wondered if you were well?' Her eyes crease in concern. 'We came by after church, but there was no answer.'

No, because we were at the garden centre in Fairleigh having lunch.

'We do *so* miss the flags in the service.'

'Oh, you miss the flags?' It comes out too quickly.

Her eyes narrow. She leans forward. I can see over her right shoulder. Gordon is in the car, parked over the road. The engine's running. It's the only noise I can hear in our quiet cul-de-sac.

'Backsliding can come upon any of us!' she whispers, fiercely. 'The days are short, remember that! Bible study Tuesday, our place, 7.30. Don't forget. Remember, a coal which is not in the fireplace soon goes cold.'

I open my mouth and find I can't say anything.

'We're praying for you.' She touches my arm with her stick fingers. 'If you want to talk, you know we're available anytime.' She gives me a tight hug, lets me go, and flashes a smile. I look at her very straight teeth. *They've got to be false.* Her eyes crease again. 'We're *family*,' she says.

Are we? I want to say it, but the words get stuck in my throat. She lingers for a moment, then rushes off down the driveway, and gets into the Corsa with a little wave. Gordon glares at me out of the driver's side window.

I shut the door. I wipe a hand over my face; my hand smells of cleaning fluid; I'm still holding the cloth. What I'd really wanted to say to her comes out in a rush: 'I don't want to read the Bible. I don't want to go to church. Don't you get it? I'm doubting *everything*!'

I sink down on the hall chair. There! I've really admitted it. Only to myself, it's true. *I doubt.* But how can I tell Anne and the rest that I'm frightened I'm losing my faith? I don't even know *why* I doubt. It's not the lawnmower – it's not the years of unanswered prayer. It's just . . . my staunch belief feels like a habit these days. I know what to say, I know how to pray. I can fool the world. But it just doesn't feel real anymore.

When I don't turn up at the Bible study, a couple of tracts are pushed through our letter box. Arthur jokes about it but I want to cry. I can't discuss *anything* with Anne and Gordon. How can I? I don't dare. I fear judgement, criticism, the shock that I am such a rubbish disciple. Or worse – maybe I'm not a Christian at all. The thought makes me tremble.

'You're a bit down, Rose,' Arthur says, that Wednesday morning. 'Why don't we go out for lunch somewhere, cheer you up?'

'Yes,' I say, flatly. 'Garden centre?'

'No, let's go to that pub in Fall's End. You know the one? With the thatched roof.'

I smile. We used to go there when we were courting. That's what we called it then. Haven't been there for years. I mean – *years.* It's only ten minutes down the road, in the next village. Why haven't we been there for so long? Then I remember. I can almost see Gordon's disapproving face.

As we turn into the car park, I feel like I've gone back in time. It's very old, with white-washed walls, like the Half Moon in Nun's Drift – not that I ever go in there. It wouldn't be *right* for a Christian lady to go in a public house, would it? What would Anne and Gordon say? *Well, they don't live in Fall's End, so they won't know, will they?*

There's a roaring fire, and a warm welcome in that little pub. I walk in, and rather than feeling uncomfortable, and wanting to pray or leave leaflets in the ladies', I feel instantly at home. Maybe that should worry me?

The pub doesn't appear to have changed since I was in my thirties. More memories. We find a table and look at the menu. It's varied, and it all looks delicious.

'Sausage and mash,' Arthur says, wistfully.

'Oh, go on,' I say, squeezing his hand across the table.

'And you?' he says, with more than a little hope in his voice, I think. 'Do you fancy the sausages, Rosey?'

He hasn't called me Rosey in a very long time. I smile. 'I'll have the halloumi.'

I enjoy my Saturdays, working in the café. I peep out of the window and see the local children finding conkers under the horse chestnut tree on the green. We did that as kids.

'Rosemary!' Meg sounds stressed. 'We've run out of butter, would you believe it? I don't suppose you could pop to the Co-op? I need to make those flapjacks next.' I turn, and she raises flour-covered hands. She's very good with scones, is Meg, and her fruit cake is very nearly as good as mine. But then, I was the one who taught her.

I swallow hard. I've started to dread meeting other members of the Fellowship in the village. Silly, really. I just don't want all the questions. I do a quick calculation. Old Mrs Fordham can't get out much anyway; Paula Bellwood works at the library in Fairleigh on Saturdays; but Mr Silent, who lives by the pub, might be cutting his front hedge, and there's always a chance that Anne and Gordon are lurking, doing a prayer walk, or shouting at the devil somewhere.

I can't live like this. I can't be afraid. I think of the grim warnings about 'backsliding' and turning away from the Lord that are appearing regularly on my front door mat. Arthur has been wonderful. He makes me laugh about it all.

I've stopped leaving the Bible open in the en suite at John 3:16, underlined and highlighted.

'Yes, of course I'll go,' I say briskly. I grab my bag and umbrella, and walk out of the shop.

It's a windy, miserable sort of day, although it doesn't deter the kids with the conkers. They're shouting with delight, finding big, shiny ones. I suddenly feel like I want to join in their innocent fun.

I keep walking. The umbrella doesn't stay up, of course. My nicely dyed blonde hair is being blown all over the place. Suddenly, I don't care. I want to jump in puddles.

I step out of the Co-op, with several packs of emergency butter. A car goes by, a new Mini. Water splashes me. I recognise the car – the Thompson-Tracey girl. I really don't like her. She has a reputation for being rude and she's certainly been rude to me before. Still, I think, observing my wet trousers, considering the circumstances, I suppose she had every right to be. But she upset Cornelia a little while ago, and I don't like that. Cornelia never told me what actually happened, but it must have been bad because she was crying. I feel cross, then shake myself. The Thompson-

Tracey girl might have dampened my trousers, but she won't dampen my day.

I don't see any of the Fellowship crowd as I walk. My thoughts turn to Anne and Gordon. I really thought Anne was my friend, but if she is, why do I feel I can't talk to her without being judged? I stop for a moment, realising I actually don't know much about Anne and Gordon at all. They've got a grown-up daughter who lives in Gloucester, but I've never seen her in the eight years I've known them. They're in rented accommodation on the new estate – all little boxes with no gardens! They haven't been there long – they used to rent a cramped semi by the Co-op and they said the upgrade was 'from the Lord'; he'd promised them their own large property next, apparently, and the fact that the new-build was in Barn Close was a sign! I wonder if they will leave the village if the Fellowship closes. *Oh, I do hope so!*

I pass the B&B on the corner of Stile Road and the flint cottage next door to it. For the first time in ages, I think about Flora Fletcher. I've known her for years, and she used to pop round for coffee once a week. Her husband – God bless his soul – was well known for his chrysanthemums. My Arthur has always been more interested in dahlias, but they used to get along, those two, at the gardening club.

Flora goes to the big church, St Saviour's, but since I came to know Anne and Gordon – who seem to think any fellowship but their own is 'heresy' – I haven't seen as much of her. I feel suddenly ashamed. Flora's a woman of quiet, gentle faith. How annoying she must have found me, bringing tracts round to her house, preaching at her, before eventually I let the friendship slide! Yet she was always kind, never unpleasant. *You know, I miss Flora.*

I reach the café, deep in thought, and then I see that Barny Baines character leaning on the counter, chatting to Meg, a cup of tea in one hand and a Bakewell tart in the other. She laughs at something he's saying. I hope she's not getting too friendly with him. He's a charmer; not the sort of man to get close to. I think of Cornelia; she was *so* obsessed with him, and I do hope that's a thing of the past. She doesn't work at the café anymore; well, she's not really needed now we've got Meg. Louisa told me that Cornelia wanted to 'move on' anyway – whatever that means. She's doing book-keeping up at the farm with her uncle, and she's started a college course. She seems keen to learn all about admin. Before she left, I told her that's how I met my husband – I was his secretary. I remember she didn't comment.

Barny looks over his shoulder and his face registers irritation as he sees me. Yes, Louisa is out, no one in the café, how *inconvenient* for me to return. *Well, tough!* Still, I have to admit, Meg really does look so much brighter these days. I hope it's nothing to do with that slimy young man.

'Don't mind me!' I exclaim, loudly, as I brush past them.

Moments later, the doorbell tinkles and I turn round and see he's gone.

'Flapjacks!' I hand Meg the butter.

We're sitting there at 4 o'clock after the quietest day the café has had in ages. The flapjacks are just about perfect, and I say so.

Meg has a lovely smile; she should do it more often. 'Well, they should be. You're a good teacher.'

A compliment! And she used to be so surly and cynical!

'Rosemary,' says Meg, setting her teacup down, her face questioning. 'Can I ask you something?'

'Of course.'

'It's about faith.'

I swallow my tea the wrong way and start to cough. She slaps me – rather brutally, I think – on the back and looks concerned. When I recover, she carries on.

'Well, I've started going to church, you see.'

Has she? I didn't know that! Louisa didn't tell me. I wonder why not.

'And the question of suffering . . . well, it's a bit massive. I wondered what you thought. That's all.' She shrugs awkwardly.

I don't know where to look. A while back, I'd have been thrilled she was asking – and I'd have had the answer – of course I would! But now . . . ?

Louisa was due back from Tony's at four. It's five-past. I stare at the door, willing Meg's aunt to walk in.

'Why does God allow suffering, Rosemary? I realise it's a big question. I mean, you know my mum and dad split up when I was a kid? That was hard. I felt so helpless. Especially when Mum moved to Canada, and I had to stay in the UK. I mean, OK, it affected me as a teenager, but it turned out alright, and I'm closer to Dad. And then there's . . .'

Yes, I know about Micky. The missing piece in Meg's puzzle. Well, I know about losing a friend, too, but not quite in the same way . . . You know, I never particularly liked that Micky – Michaela, to give her the proper label. I remember her coming to Nun's Drift with Meg and her father. She was a pretty girl; Arthur called her 'winsome'. But I found her insolent; there was always a mocking expression in her eyes. No. I didn't like Micky at all.

'Honestly,' I say at last. 'I really don't know.' I push a lot of flapjack into my mouth so I don't have to say anything further.

'Jason says it shouldn't be like this. He says human beings were friends with God and then it all went wrong, and suffering's just part of that. Do you think that's true?'

Jason? Oh – the young vicar. The Anglican boy.

'Hmm. Mmm.' I send up a quick prayer to a God I'm no longer sure exists. *Please, let someone come in the café!*

She leans across the table, earnestly. 'You see, if I can believe that, I think I can cope more with an imperfect world.'

'Mmm . . .' I stand up quickly, brush a few imaginary crumbs from my cashmere top, and stare at the door again. *Louisa, come back! Anyone! Please, please, let someone come in!*

She keeps talking. 'Is that how you see it, then? That it shouldn't really be like this, but somehow God's in it with us?'

I look down at her. Right, time for some truth.

'I don't know. Prayers aren't always answered,' I say, shortly. 'Life isn't easy.'

She looks at me quizzically and I suddenly realise how awful that sounds. I have good health, a comfortable lifestyle, a lovely home and a wonderful husband who has put up with me all these years when all I have tried to do is force him to believe something he really doesn't.

'Do you have doubts, then, Rosemary?'

'Yes,' I reply, frankly. 'Just lately, I find that I do.'

She nods, slowly, and tells me that she thinks I'm brave for admitting it. *Brave?* Is that really what she thinks? I'd expected disappointment. I'm about to tell her the full depth of my doubt, but then I wonder how much that will help this questioning soul. I feel hot and panicky. Then the door slams open and a couple of very damp cyclists walk in. Literally, I've been saved by the bell. I dismiss the thought that it's an answer to prayer. I rush to serve them.

I'm cleaning out the cupboard in the hall. That's what I do on Sunday mornings now. I clean and tidy. I find it very relaxing.

This cupboard is full of things I really don't need, and I'm absorbed in what I do. Discarded plates – they'll need a wash – a couple of my mother's china ornaments and old vases that can go to a charity shop. Behind these, there are old bus tickets – I ask you! – in a copper bowl, and some very crinkly old conkers (that makes me smile), a jigsaw puzzle, brand new, never touched, and right at the back, under a pile of dusters, a half-finished cross-stitch that Arthur bought me long ago. *Oh, how I used to love cross-stitch!*

When was the last time I cleared out this cupboard? It must have been years ago. Eight years, ten? We've been in the bungalow for twenty. Some of these things might have been there that long!

I look at the cross-stitch. Why didn't I finish it? Too busy . . . walking the boundaries of the village, praying, stopping anyone I could to tell them about heaven and how to get there, asking people to tea just so I could invite them to the Fellowship. I feel suddenly breathless.

I sink down on the floor, with my back to the cupboard, resting against one of the doors, which shuts with a 'click'. And I see my life has become just like this cupboard. It's a picture of my faith. My life has become cluttered with *stuff.* So much so that the important things have been shoved away. They've been swamped, lost, rejected. I'm clutching the cross-stitch in my hand. A rose. Not just my name, but a symbol of love.

I remember the day Arthur gave it to me. It was my birthday. The first birthday I'd had in the bungalow. I was thirty-nine. Everything seemed simpler then; anything seemed possible. It was before I lost the hope of ever having children of my own, before my father developed dementia, before my dear friend Lizzy was killed in that terrible accident.

It was Lizzy's death that got me into it, really − church. It was that stained-glass window in St Saviour's, here in Nun's Drift. I was attending the funeral, and I was so heartbroken, especially for her husband and young daughter. Then, when it threatened to become too unbearable, I'd spotted these marvellous colours, rich and glorious, and a shepherd holding a little lamb, and underneath the words in a scroll: 'The Good Shepherd'. It stuck with me. I did a bit of investigating. It seemed to come from a passage in the Gospel of John and was about Jesus Christ. There was a woman at work who caught me one day reading the Gospel − I'd bought a Bible by then − and explained to me that she was a Baptist, and would I like to go to church with her? Well, not really, but there was a lunchtime service on

Thursdays at Fairleigh Baptist Church, round the corner from the office, so one day I went with her. I loved it. I felt there really *was* a Good Shepherd looking after me; he understood, he cared. It was a great comfort.

Then the years rolled on, and I prayed for a child, and the child didn't come. And later, I prayed for my father, for healing. He died last January. He hadn't recognised me in years.

I jerk my mind back to when I first believed. I'd found new purpose. Later I met Anne and Gordon, and felt they were kindred spirits in my zeal and fervour, teaching me so much I didn't know before. Bible studies, prayer groups, I went to them all; and somewhere, in all the busyness, even the Good Shepherd himself was pushed to the back of the cupboard.

I can't cry, but my breathing is heavy and difficult. How I wish I could find the Shepherd again; that acceptance and comfort from Someone who loved me, even though he knew all my faults and failings . . .

'I'm so sorry.' That's all I can manage to stutter.

'Are you alright, Rosey, love?' There's Arthur's concerned face. He helps me get to my feet – not that easy these days, I really do eat too many of my own cakes – and gives me a cuddle. Words from the Bible spring to mind about love never failing, holding no record of any wrong. *That's my Arthur.* Suddenly it comes to me: yes, maybe that's my Shepherd too.

'Let's get a cup of tea,' Arthur suggests, softly, 'and maybe a slice of your chocolate cake.'

'I found this,' I manage to say, showing him the cross-stitch. His face brightens as he remembers it.

It's on the arm of my chair, later, as we sit companionably together.

I put my glasses on, get the needle and thread, and start work.

It's stopped raining, and the autumn sun makes the leaves of the maple tree nearby look as if they're on fire. I pull the gate shut behind me. I feel content. I've written a note and put it through Anne's door. It's my formal resignation from the Fellowship. I don't say why I'm going, and I'm not discourteous. I just say that's it, goodbye, God bless.

My phone buzzes as I head for home. It's a message from Anne. Nothing to say 'we're sorry'. She just says thanks for letting them know, and asks if she can have the flags.

I'm not sure how I feel. Hurt? Annoyed? I breathe deeply. Then I have a thought. There's time before I get Arthur's tea; he always goes to his gardening club on Monday afternoons, so he won't be back quite yet. I hurry up the hill to St Saviour's. I cast a furtive glance over my shoulder and then stop myself; it doesn't matter if Anne and Gordon see me. *I don't care.*

I creak open the little lychgate and start crunching up the gravel path. I wonder if the door's locked, but there's only one way to find out. Then I hear it. Crying.

There's a dark-haired girl sat in the porch. I see who it is. Alexandra Thompson-Tracey. Oh dear.

I'm about to scurry away when she looks up at me out of big, grey, tear-filled eyes. They remind me of someone, and I take a deep breath. She recognises me and looks embarrassed. She fumbles in her pocket but doesn't find a tissue, then wipes her tears away brusquely with the back of her hand.

I dither. But then, rather than walking away (and believe me, that's what I want to do), I find myself almost propelled to sit beside her. Oddly, she doesn't tell me to leave her alone in that barking voice I've heard around the village for so many years.

'It's Alexandra, isn't it?'

She doesn't answer. I find some tissues in my bag – unused – and hand them to her. She takes them and blows her nose. I keep quiet, and start to feel very uncomfortable. I wonder if I can excuse myself politely.

'Ally,' she says, gruffly.

For a moment I wonder what she's talking about. Then I realise she's introducing herself. Before I can say anything, she speaks, abruptly.

'You knew my mother.'

I nod. 'She was my best friend.'

She sighs – a deep, heart-breaking sigh. Without thinking, I start to pray, in my heart – genuinely, truthfully – for this obviously broken girl whose mother meant so much to me.

'I was away at school when it happened,' she says, dully.

'Yes,' I say.

'When I came home, Daddy couldn't talk to me. Next holidays, Bella was there.' Her lip curls. 'And that was that.'

'I expect your father was lonely,' I offer, tentatively.

'We're all lonely,' she says, bluntly. She's twisting the tissues and I start to worry about the mess she'll make in the porch. But really . . . what does that matter? She sniffs loudly. 'Nobody cares, and that's how life is.'

I speak slowly. 'I think Someone does care, actually . . .'

She shoots me a look that says, 'Oh, don't start on about God! Everyone in the village knows you're a religious nut!'

I swallow. Dare I say anything further? *Yes.* I persist, gently but firmly. 'I didn't think he did . . . care, I mean. The Good Shepherd. But just lately I've been thinking maybe he *does* care after all. Just a thought, you know?'

Her face is impassive, hard to read. She sniffs again.

I hand her another tissue. She takes it. 'Anyway,' I say, 'it's interesting you came to his house when you were upset.'

'I just wanted to get out of the rain,' she replies, sharply.

Oh . . . She was visiting the grave.

I'll see the stained-glass window another day. As I get up to leave, I hear her voice.

'What was she like?'

She's looking at me with haughty yet vulnerable eyes.

'She was wonderful,' I reply, warmly. 'She was fun, and always laughing . . . she had a great sense of humour. I loved her. So did your dad. Love at first sight.'

A slight, sad smile cracks the frosty mask.

A thought drops into my mind. I dismiss it. It comes back. I don't really want to do this, but I'll give it a try.

'I was looking through some old photo albums the other day. There are pictures of your mum when she was young.' I take a deep breath. 'Would you like to see them?'

I don't know who is more surprised by my invitation, her or me. She stares. I expect a curt response. It doesn't come.

'Yes,' she says, at last. 'Yes, I would.' Then she mutters, almost inaudibly, 'Thank you.'

Bella's jam really is the best, and it goes so nicely with clotted cream. I'm sure it doesn't do me any good, but it's just so tasty.

I turn the sign round: 'Closed' and shut the door, the scone in my other hand. Another day over.

Meg is leaning on the counter, texting someone. I hope it's not that awful Barny, but who knows. Louisa is busy in the kitchen. I've noticed she's been quiet lately. I wonder if she's getting cold feet about the wedding; after all, she's never been married before. I'll have to find time to have a little chat with her.

Meg looks up and smiles.

'Messaging your boyfriend?' I ask, pointedly.

'No, it's Jason. The vicar.'

'Oh yes?' My voice is knowing.

'No, no. Nothing like that. Jason's just a friend.'

Hmm. Well, a vicar has got to be a better bet than that smarmy handyman. Something two-faced about him . . . I wouldn't trust him. On the other hand, Meg is no fool.

'There's a get-together in the Half Moon tonight for the little group that's been meeting on Monday evenings,' she's saying. 'We're all new to this faith thing. That old geezer who lives by the pub started coming.'

'What, Mr Silent?' I can't help but exclaim. She laughs, and I put my hand to my cheek. 'Oh, that's awful of me. So sorry.'

'His name's Alec.'

I know that, actually. Arthur knows him from the gardening club.

'He asks loads of questions. He says he's been in churches for years and never really understood you can have an actual friendship with Jesus.'

'Well!' I can't think of anything else to say.

'I think I'm beginning to believe in it, Rosemary,' says Meg, slowly. 'Or believe in *him*.'

'You hold onto him, dear,' I say. My voice sounds too fervent, but I can't help it. 'Just you hold onto the Good Shepherd.'

She puts her head to one side and looks at me questioningly. 'Last time we spoke, you seemed to have doubts?'

'I did. Maybe we all do at times. Get our eyes off him, go off in all sorts of directions, even if sometimes we think those directions are good.' I pat her hand. 'Thankfully, he has a way of finding us when we're lost.'

The whole topic of 'losing' isn't a great one to bring up with Meg, and I feel sorry I used that wording. She sees my expression.

'Don't worry,' she says, softly. 'It's OK.'

And I know it is.

I'm cutting the sandwiches, piling the plates high. I go into the living room and hand Arthur his tea.

'Ham?' He looks surprised.

'Finest Wiltshire!' I brandish one of my own sandwiches. 'Delicious.'

'It really is!' he says, taking a bite.

I hand him a packet of crisps. 'Smoky bacon?'

He starts to laugh. I laugh too.

'Did the young lady have a lovely time, looking at the pictures?'

'Oh yes.' I settle in my chair. 'I've asked her to come to tea on Wednesday. Is that alright? And Flora Fletcher – remember her? I popped round to her place and invited her for coffee.' I smile at the thought. 'She's coming here next Tuesday.'

'That's nice,' he says, through a mouthful of sandwich.

I glance up at the finished rose cross-stitch, pride of place above the mantelpiece.

'It's looking good, Rosey,' says Arthur.

I nod. 'Yes, Arthur. It is!'

PART FOUR

Jason's Story

Perspectives

I wake up with a start. My heart is hammering against my rib cage. I'm too frightened to open my eyes. *He's here. In the room. I can feel the darkness.*

Slowly, slowly, I start to breathe normally. It was a dream; just a dream, that's all. I fumble for the bedside light and switch it on. My phone tells me it's 3 a.m.

This old vicarage is great, but it's big, and in winter, it's freezing. The central heating won't creak on until 7 a.m. It's too cold to get up and make a drink.

Come on, Jason. It was just a dream.

That reminds me of another voice: *Come on, Jason. It was just a joke.*

It soon became: *Come on, Jason. I'm teaching you to be a man.*

Only his idea of being a man was to beat up his girlfriend's son.

I know I ought to pray, but I can't. All the fears are flooding back. Old, taunting words. *Not good enough. You'll never belong. You're useless. You don't fit in.*

I reach for a book of sudokus I keep by my bed, and that takes my mind off things. Its 5 a.m. before I switch the light off and fall into a troubled sleep. When I wake again, I'm in need of a strong coffee.

Flora Fletcher turns up later with some homemade cake. She does a bit of cleaning for me. I really appreciate that lemon drizzle.

'I didn't know you baked,' I say.

'I don't. Rosemary made it. I can't eat it all, and Barny said he thought you'd finish it up. So . . .'

'Oh, did he?' I laugh. Good to break the tension.

'Yes, and don't let that wretched cat get it.'

The cat – which I inherited from the previous incumbent, and which Flora doesn't like – opens a lazy eye from his favourite position by the window.

'You know what happened when he got your liquorice allsorts!' With that warning, she closes the door to my study.

The cat's asleep again and I finish the cake, looking out at the heavy grey skies that threaten rain. Probably cold enough for sleet. Such a busy time of year, Advent.

The sleet starts as I'm reviewing the list before me. I'm part of a team, and this is my first parish. The team are great. There's Kathy from St Mary's, Fall's End, Mark from the Howfields – my friend and spiritual director – and Ash over at Smith's Common. Denise is the boss, she's at St Peter's in Fairleigh; pretty high church, not quite my style; which is why (I think) a couple of my parishioners have moved over there – Flora mentioned there were nervous comments like 'Does he play a guitar?' when I first arrived. I guess I'm too informal for some, although we have a variety of services at St Saviour's – formal and relaxed. I've got a plan to start a café-style church in the spring; might appeal to the young families in the new-builds. I'll have a chat with Louisa about that.

In front of me is a list of people I try to pray for every day. Right now, I'm concentrating on Tony and Louisa. They're getting married in February, but she came to me a while back with a few concerns. She's always been able to offload on me, right from my very first day, when I went into the teashop to introduce myself. Strange, really, because she doesn't come to church – apart from weddings, funerals, and once when she got stuck up the bell tower after a bit of 'exploring'. But she was worried. At that time, worried about her niece, Meg; yes, I prayed for Meg for some time before I met her in person.

Anyway, on this occasion, it was only after she'd talked about a few very minor issues that I was able to cut to the heart of the matter. Tony drinks.

I sit back as sleet lashes the windows. I look out again. The oak tree beyond my hedge, naked of leaves, is staunch and tough, but the way the branches are bending is quite breath-taking. If it didn't have good roots, that tree would topple over – the amount of rain and wind we've had.

I don't miss the parallel, and jot it down in my notebook; something for a future sermon. Standing, I look further, out across the fields one way, to the poplar trees on the edge of the village. The other way, down the hill, I can see houses, the roofs, thatched and slate, standing firm against the elements.

Barny's always got his bag packed. You know that, don't you? He's ready to leave anytime.

I try to quieten the voice in my head. *He meets with me regularly. He comes to the men's group in Fairleigh.*

Right back at me: *Yeah, he likes the company.*

I shake my head. *Yes, but he's been to one or two of the Monday evening meetings.*

The negative voice again: *He only comes because of Meg.*

My stomach lurches. *That's not true.*

I lean my arm against the wall, fixing my eyes on the distant poplars. Meg is starting to ask real questions about faith. She's really opening up on Mondays. When I first asked her if she had any questions, she'd quizzed me on who the nun was. I'd said, bewildered, 'What nun?' *Nun's Drift!* Of course. Anyway, not quite the question I was expecting. I hadn't got a clue and I think she found that amusing. I said I'd check it out, and I'd discovered it was something to do with the nunnery that used to be on the edge of the village. It's four cottages now. Nothing else is known. Or at least, not by me.

After that, the questions got more serious. Recently, she told me she was praying for Rosemary Lane to come to the Christmas services. *Rosemary!* I saw her recently, coming out of the church on a Thursday morning. I was just walking in to take the little service for people who can't get to church on Sundays. She'd looked rather surprised to see me, which was weird, considering I'm the vicar and I was all robed up.

'Oh, lovely to see you. Rosemary, isn't it?'

'Mmm. Lovely. Yes. Err . . . Yes. Thank you.'

Awkward silence.

'There's a short quiet service in a minute. Just reflecting on the coming Advent season. Would you like to join?'

'Um – er – well, no. I mean – sorry, I'm really busy. Thank you.'

She'd scurried off down the path like a scared rabbit. I'd smiled and shaken my head. I know she'd left the Fellowship, the odd little gathering in the hall, but that's closed down now anyway. The couple running the group are leaving the village. I didn't know much about them; I met them once – they were putting leaflets through doors – and invited them for a meal, but they hadn't been interested. Afterwards, I'd had a couple of brightly coloured tracts shoved through my letter box about where religious institutions had got it all wrong, the usual stuff. I'd added Anne and Gordon Ward to my prayer list. Which I really must get back to.

I need to pray for Meg. She's found some peace about her friend Micky, a girl she's fondly described as a bit of a free spirit, and is hopefully shouldering less of the blame for her disappearance. Anyway, we've been praying together earnestly that Micky will be found. We often sit in this very study – door open, of course, and only when Flora is here – and talk. Sometimes I meet her in the pub. Not too frequently.

'It's snowing, Vicar.'

I was going to say, drily, that I didn't think it was manna from heaven floating past my window, but Flora's face is shining. She's mid-sixties, but she looks like a little kid today.

'Do you want to go and build a snowman?' I laugh.

'You know, I just might.'

What is it about snow that gets people so excited?

She shuts the door behind her, and I hear the drone of the vacuum cleaner in the hallway. It goes quiet, and I hear the frenetic ring! ring! of the doorbell. There's some frantic knocking too. I stand up and offer a quick prayer. Someone's in trouble.

Meg shoots into the study, with Flora trailing behind her a little helplessly. Meg's covered in snow; her coat is dripping on the worn Axminster carpet. Her nose is rather a cute red, and her face is glowing. I stop myself from admiring her, it's not very professional. Anyway, she's not here for a social call – is she? Her eyes are dancing and she laughs more freely than I've seen before.

'Jason, Jason! They've found her. They've found Micky.'

The wonderful Flora has produced some buttered toast, and Meg and I are sitting by the little coal fire in the study, as snow flutters past the window and settles on the ledge. It has covered the garden and the fields like icing sugar.

A cup of tea and some toast is Flora's answer to life's every crisis. Barny – who lodges with her – often tells me how she tries to feed him up, while ruefully patting his stomach. There's no excess weight on him, so she clearly isn't succeeding. *New Year's resolution, Jason. Cut out the cakes.*

Meg has taken her boots off and is toasting her toes by the fire. Flora looks at me with raised eyebrows when she asks if any more tea is required.

'No thanks,' says Meg. 'I must be going in a minute.'

She's excited, she's thrilled, she's nervous. Micky is alive! She has been in contact with her parents. There aren't too many details, but it looks as if Micky is coming home. Her parents have been in touch with Meg's dad. They're so excited, he says they're 'beside themselves'. I smile at the notion that there's no thought of condemnation, of telling the girl about the pain she has caused. *Another sermon. Quite a good one, too.*

Meg talks to me about the overwhelming desire to go and 'put things right' with her friend. I say I think she needs to be patient. Does Micky *want* to meet her? I suggest she exercises caution; it's about what her friend wants, not what Meg needs. I encourage her to try to see things from Micky's perspective. I try to sound impartial, but it's not easy.

She takes my advice well, and nods in understanding. 'Jason, I'm so grateful for all your support in this, and for everyone . . . and I'm *really* grateful to God.'

I want to warn her – I think of the growing freedom, evident in her face and countenance. *Please, Meg, if you speak to her, if you go to see her, don't put on any old mantle of condemnation that might be waiting.* I don't say it, though, because she's beaming not with the effects of the cold, but with sheer happiness.

She puts her boots back on at the door, and before she leaves, she throws her arms around my neck and gives me a hug.

I wish she hadn't done that.

'You know your problem . . .' Not sure I need advice from Barny Baines, but on the other hand, who knows? I glance at him as I drink my real ale. 'You take life too seriously.'

'Yeah, they kind of teach you that at vicar school,' I reply.

There's a loud laugh from the window seat and we both turn to see what the commotion is all about. It's Tony, there for his lunchtime refreshment, larger than life, as ever.

Barny turns back to the bar. 'You know he drinks too much?'

I say nothing. Louisa catches my eye.

The door opens, and people walk in, stamping boots and scattering snow everywhere. I'm glad of the massive, roaring fire. With all the old beams in the pub, and the big fir tree in the corner decorated with gold and silver tinsel, it's like something from a Christmas card.

Tony gets up and winds his way over to me. He puts his glass down next to my hand and slaps me on the shoulder. It takes a moment or two to get my breath back.

'Look at that, Vicar,' he says proudly. 'Non-alcoholic ale, and I can still have a good ol' laugh. What do you think of *that* then, eh?' He leans close to me. 'I can give it up anytime.'

I wonder if he knows he's lying.

One of the people who just walked in comes up to the bar.

'Oh, hello, young Ally,' says Tony, noticing her.

Who could miss her, in that fake fur hat and tight leggings? She glances at me. I nod, she nods. Clearly we're on nodding terms. I've only spoken to her a couple of times; once when I called on her father and stepmother when I was new to the parish. Her father was friendly, vague and awkward, and her stepmother looked as if she couldn't wait for me to leave. Ally had popped her head round the drawing room door and said hello, and that was that.

She was friendlier a few weeks ago when I met her at the firework celebration on the village green. There was the usual hubbub around an enormous bonfire, and the enticing smell of burgers and onions sent me strolling over to a nearby van. We were in a short queue; she'd been grabbing a couple of coffees and turned round so quickly that she bumped into me. No damage done, no coffee spilt. She'd managed a smile and an apology before she darted away. Someone muttered that she usually swore and barked, and 'you ought to be glad, Vicar, she'd have blamed you for knocking into her if you weren't a man of God'. As I watched her disappear into the crowd that cold evening, under the canopy of real stars and fake flashes, I had a feeling Ally Thompson-Tracey didn't care much about God or anyone else. But that was judgemental – and based on village gossip. Remembering this now isn't helpful; I say sorry to the Boss in my mind.

'Hello, Tony.' She has a cut-glass accent. She ignores Barny completely, gets her drink and goes back to her friends.

'Hello, Tony,' mocks Barny into his beer.

'That's not kind,' I tell him.

'Shut that door, will you?' shouts someone at the latest arrival. 'Keep the heat in!'

I turn and watch Meg as she walks up to the bar. So does Barny.

'Want a drink?' he says quickly, before I can offer.

'Thank you. Gingerbread latte would be nice.'

He rolls his eyes. 'Never going to get you drunk, am I?'

I feel like a bystander in a little play. I make my excuses and follow Tony back to his table. Louisa says hello and we have a brief chat. Meg doesn't join us, she's too busy talking to Barny. I have ungracious thoughts about him. *See? You're just not good enough, Jason.*

Time to leave.

On the way back to the vicarage, I notice Arthur, Rosemary's husband – seen him around the village but never spoken apart from a brief 'Good morning'. He's clearing snow from the path of the house next door to the pub. The owner, Alec, is watching from the door. I remember he's had a bad cold this week. There's a spare shovel leaning against the hedge. I grab it. Amazing how physical work focuses the mind.

I love Advent: hope, peace, love, joy. I'm preaching from Galatians 5, and the church is pretty full. I don't like to keep staring, but she's right at the front and I'm really pleased. Rosemary has come to church with Flora. I notice she keeps looking up at that stained-glass window, the one with the Shepherd and the lamb in his arms. I want to talk to her about that, she's staring at it so intently.

Hope is such a great topic to speak about. I have plenty of hope as I shake hands with Rosemary at the door. As she crunches off down the path, so kindly cleared of snow by Barny, she stops, says something to Flora, and turns back. I shake a few more hands and then step aside to talk to her.

'It was so good to hear all about hope,' she says. 'Hope because Jesus died for us. Hope for eternity. Hope that God answers prayers. In his own time, in his own way. I suppose we have to trust that, don't we? That he knows best.'

Her statement is more of a question, really. I can see the hope in her eyes.

'Yes,' I say confidently. 'I think so.'

'Can you pray for someone?' she asks, suddenly.

'Kind of in the job description.'

She leans forward and whispers the name. 'Ally Thompson-Tracey. I knew her mother. We've sort of become friends. But she's not a happy girl.'

I nod. 'On the list.'

Meg appears, laughing with one of the elderly ladies from the congregation.

'Jason! It's so good. I've had an email from Micky's mum.' She grabs my arm and I feel panic rising. 'She's been abroad. And she got married! That's why they couldn't find her. She's—'

'Ah, Mrs Fordham! So good to see you.' I give the old lady such a welcome she seems surprised.

Meg is behind me. 'Can I talk to you later?'

'I've got a pastoral visit.' I turn and take a step backwards, raising a hand as I smile and head back into the church. 'Speak soon.'

I glance over my shoulder. I don't miss the wounded expression on her face.

I'm in the vestry, disrobing, when there's a knock at the door. I groan. *Please, not Meg.*

Barny doesn't wait for me to say, 'Come in.' He grins. 'I cleared the snow.'

'Oh, yes, so I saw. Thanks.'

'You look a bit stressed. Fancy a pint?'

'No, I have a pastoral visit.' I realise how terse that seems. 'Sorry. I might, later.'

He raises his eyebrows.

'Anyway, where were you?' I ask. He doesn't do services. *Yet.*

'Lurking around, as ever.' He grins again. He's a good-looking fella. No wonder there's been women trouble around him. He looks serious, all of a sudden. 'You heard about this Micky turning up? Well, obviously, I suppose.' He coughs, and shuffles his feet on the cold stone. 'Married, separated and pregnant. A reason to come home, I guess. You know, I think Meg's—'

I look at my phone. 'Sorry, Barny—'

'Pastoral visit, yep. See you later.'

I should feel guilty about lying to them both. I breathe out, slowly. I had another nightmare last night. I need to relax. I'm getting a bit of a headache. Is my throat sore? I hope I'm not coming down with anything. I always seem to catch the local viruses.

The churchwarden is whistling in the porch as I leave, sweeping up old leaves. The air is bracing, although the snow has stopped. It'll freeze tonight.

I'm shivering. I should feel well fortified by Flora's chicken soup ('Not homemade, Vicar. Out of a tin. Sorry!') – I seem to have consumed bucket-loads of it. But I wonder, as I stare at the woman in front of me, whether I'm feeling the after-effects of the virus, or whether the slight shakiness is due to something else.

'So,' she's saying, in a matter-of-fact voice, 'I'm going.'

'OK.' Seeing Meg wasn't planned. I've bumped into her as I was coming out of the village store. She's with Tony's niece.

'We'll pray for you,' I say, 'after the morning service tomorrow, if you like.'

I hope my voice is dispassionate. I've put her off twice this week, using illness as an excuse – well, not an excuse really . . . I *have* been sick. She'd wanted to talk. Clearly, this is what she wanted to talk about.

'Well,' she says. 'They prayed for me on Monday at the group. We all missed you, Jason.'

'Ah, man flu.' I laugh a bit, and brandish a packet of cough sweets I've just bought.

'Should you be outside? You're a bit pale, like,' Cornelia points out.

'I'm on the mend,' I assure her.

She doesn't look convinced. 'You need 'oney and lemon, with a bit of ginger in it, I reckon. You eatin' alright?'

'Flora looks after me.'

'Oh yes, Barny's landlady,' Meg says.

Cornelia immediately looks at the ground. Meg flushes slightly.

'Anyway,' Meg goes on, quickly, 'I'm leaving on Monday. Micky wants to see me, so I have to take that chance. I don't know what I can say ... apologies don't seem enough ...'

'Well, remember what we were talking about in the group recently? Leave space for silence. Let God speak.'

'Thank you, Jason,' says Meg, warmly. 'You've been such a wonderful help in all this.'

I pull my hood up. It's started to snow again.

'I'm a bit scared.' She shakes her head. 'Actually, that's an understatement.'

'Yes, well, it's a big deal and has been for a long time ...' My words trail away into the cold air.

She looks up at me. She has such expressive green eyes. 'I hope to be back for Christmas. But obviously, I want to spend time with my dad too.'

'I hope the trains are running.' *Do I?*

'You'll miss Nun's Drift, Meg, won't you?' Cornelia squints against the chilly gusts. 'Even the bell-ringin'?' She grins, and Meg laughs a little.

'Don't you like the bells?' I ask her. 'I didn't know ...'

'Well, they're ...'

'You *are* coming back?' I blurt out, suddenly. I'm surprised at the forcefulness. Meg seems surprised too.

'I'm . . . look, I'll keep in touch.' She sounds unsure now. 'Is that OK?'

'Fine. Of course.' As I walk away, hands deep in pockets, I make a mental note to not check emails after 9 o'clock in the evening.

Boundaries.

My latest sermon – delivered in a slightly croaky voice – was about peace. But I feel little peace this morning. My stomach's churning – another bad night.

We'd prayed for Meg on Sunday, after the service, and there were lots of tears. I handed out a few platitudes but really, I felt I was out of my depth with so much emotion. I thought maybe I wasn't quite myself after being ill. I wanted to offer comfort, but in the end, I let Rosemary do it; she prayed for peace. *Jason, you just preached on that. Couldn't you have prayed for it?*

I can see Rosemary becoming a bit of a rock in the church, if she keeps on attending. She did some pastoral visits when I couldn't manage it due to man flu. Daisy Parker from the clothes shop has been quite unwell, so Rosemary took her some homemade meals. She even visited the woman who runs the antique shop when she sprained her ankle – a bit haughty, not the friendliest of people. The curate from Fairleigh was meant to come and give me a hand while I was out of action, but he'd slipped on the ice and broken his collarbone. Weird that we can be short-staffed in God's kingdom.

Anyway, Meg left yesterday. She'd sent an email in the morning, saying she was nervous. *Meg – don't pick up what you've put down. Remember forgiveness.*

I sit back, and rub my hand over my face. The clock ticks, the cat stretches. Then it comes to me, quietly, like a whisper: *Listen to your own words, Jason! You have to forgive yourself. Even for the time you left a mess in your mother's hallway . . .*

I recall telling Meg about visiting the past and not living there. And yet, how easy it is to slip back; I see a picture in my mind of the churchwarden, sweeping up old, dry leaves. *Yesterday's rubbish . . . keeps on swirling around.*

There's a beep. I look at my phone. Tony wants to meet me in the Half Moon. I should insist on meeting at the vicarage, but somehow, I just don't have the strength.

He's there, leaning on the bar when I go in. He has a drink – it looks like apple juice. He brings it over to the table by the window, and we settle there. I notice the snow is turning to slush in the road outside. Beautiful white, turned grey and blotched and dirty.

'I drink too much, Vicar, you know that.' He sits back in his seat. 'But I'm on the wagon, as they say.' Then he adds, almost under his breath, 'Just hope I can stay there.'

'You can get help.'

He shrugs. 'I started drinking when my missus left me. But then Lou . . . Anyway, it helps having Corny about. She never lets me get away with anything.'

'Yes, how is Cornelia? I used to see her around the village, but not so much lately. Although I saw her with Meg, outside the shop . . .' Even saying her name makes my heart flip about. 'Is she OK?'

'Oh yeah, she's doing this course. She likes admin and all that.' He drinks his fruit juice and pulls a face. 'And it keeps her out of harm's way.'

I really shouldn't listen to village gossip, but it's no secret that Cornelia had a huge crush on Barny. I take a sip of my real ale.

'Anyhow, it's not my problem now, is it? More Lou's, really.' He rolls his eyes. 'Mind you, I reckon Meg can take care of herself. She's been around. My Corny hasn't.'

Been around?

He nods. 'Meg don't look it, but she's tough alright.'

What exactly does that mean?

'I was a bit worried about Corny, to tell the truth. But she's throwing herself into work, and this admin course. Making some new friends and all that, at the college over in Fairleigh. She's much happier. She's naïve, you see. A dreamer. She's been a bit sheltered. It'll do her good to have a wider perspective on life.'

Perspectives again.

'Look, I've got to talk to you.' He leans across the table and I instinctively lean back. He's a big man. 'I've – look. I've been married, right? And I've lived with someone. That was Roseanne. Yes?'

'OK,' I say, slowly.

His voice is low. 'Well, my wife left me. Then Roseanne cleared off. Right?'

'Right.'

'Well, what's to stop it happening again, then? Eh? I'm not an easy bloke to live with. Lou knows me – known me for years. But ...'

We have a little chat about the nature of trust and commitment. I feel a complete fraud. A real hypocrite. I manage to sound professional, and Tony listens to what I say. I point out that stopping the heavy drinking is a good move. I'm careful how I word it ... if he needs more help in that area, he needs to get it. Pre-marriage counselling is a must, too, in my opinion. He looks doubtful.

'The vicar over at Fairleigh does a good marriage course,' I tell him. 'You need to sign up.'

'Look, I'm not the sort to talk about feelings, Vicar.'

I down the last of my real ale. 'You're talking to me.'

'Yeah, well, you've become a bit of a mate, haven't you? You're like a normal guy. Oh – sorry.' He scratches his head. 'I just mean, you're not like a proper vicar. Oh, that came out wrong—' He shrugs his massive shoulders. 'I don't usually do the whole religious thing. Ain't my bag. But Lou says she wants to start going to church. It's all your fault. You've got into Meg's head and she's got her aunty all interested in God and all that. Anyway, Lou thinks you're alright...'

I'm in Meg's head?

'I think you need to go to Denise in Fairleigh,' I say. 'She and her husband, Ted, run the course. It's very good.'

'Aw, a lady priest...'

'Drag yourself into the twenty-first century,' I suggest. 'It might help.'

Tony sits back, suddenly. 'My old man used to say it's better never to marry than to marry the wrong person.'

'I think he was right.' I glance out of the window at the slush. 'Doubts are natural, Tony.' I think of something godly to say. *I've done hope. I've done peace. Next sermon is on love.* My voice is confident. 'Louisa loves you. That's obvious.'

He sounds unsure. 'Is it?'

I'm surprised by his apparent uncertainty. 'Well – yes! And you love her, don't you?'

He doesn't answer directly. He averts his gaze. 'So . . . What *is* love, then, eh?'

'Well, I'm talking about it on Sunday, as a matter of fact.' I cough. 'John 3:16 says—'

'No, I mean, what *is* it?' He looks at me now. 'Don't give me all that vicar stuff.'

I feel my confidence draining away. 'Um – well, it's preferring someone else over yourself, isn't it?'

'You're asking me?' He roars with laughter. When the laughter subsides, he says, in a more subdued tone, 'I'd do anything for her, I want to look after her, and I want her to be happy. So I guess that about covers it, doesn't it?'

'Yes . . . I guess it does.'

'What about you, then? You're not married.'

'Is love just confined to marriage? There are different types of love. Love is sacrifice. Love is—'

'Yeah, come on – a partner! Ever think about it?'

'No, I don't.' I shouldn't have been so abrupt. I grip my empty glass with two hands. 'Sorry . . . I just made a vow. To be celibate. That's all.'

'A what to be what?' His eyes widen.

I laugh a little. 'I promised God I wouldn't get into a romantic relationship. Dedicated myself to God. That's it.'

'You're joking!' He looks stunned. 'That's a bit extreme! Why d'you do that?' he adds, mystified. 'I mean, that's a Catholic thing, isn't it?'

'Not always.'

He blows his cheeks out. 'I admire you. I couldn't do it.'

No. Not many people can.

'I mean, everyone wants a family, don't they? Somewhere they belong?'

It's a statement. He doesn't expect an answer.

I was twenty-two years old when I came to faith. I think about that day as I trudge home. Dirty snow is piled at the side of the road. I remember the guys coming to the gym, chatting to us about God. Somehow, I just believed. Changed the way I thought about life – the way I thought about myself. *I'm known. I'm loved.* No father's name on my birth certificate, it felt good to know that my identity wasn't dependent on someone I never knew.

The beatings had stopped when I beefed up. Anyway, eventually Mum saw through the guy and found the strength to boot him out, with me at her side, after that last time, in her hallway . . . Didn't stop her getting involved with someone else almost immediately, though. He was another one who didn't have boundaries. Only this one shouted and didn't use his fists.

I met my partner shortly after I moved out. It felt so good to be loved. Only it wasn't love, was it? It was toxic. Control. Manipulation.

The God guys came at just the right time. I walked out of my partner's arms into the arms of God. I totally believed Jesus paid the price for me to be right with God, all my shame, all of it, nailed to the cross. How could I do anything but give him the rest of my life? I remember how gladly I shut the door to relationships forever.

I'm happy with my decision. I'm at peace with it.

Aren't I?

It hits me like a wet snowball. *How much have I sacrificed? Was it for God? Or was it for me? Have I just chosen a way to avoid intimacy altogether, because I couldn't handle it?* Tony's words echo in my mind: 'Everyone wants a family, don't they? Somewhere they belong?' *What have I given up? And for who, and for what...? And what happens when you meet someone and unexpectedly your inner world is turned upside down? Does that invalidate your promise? Oh, Jason! You should have been more careful.*

I need to talk to my mentor, Mark. *I'll call him as soon as...*

'You OK?' A female voice cuts through the winter air. 'You're dithering on the kerb. You afraid of getting your feet wet?'

Ally Thompson-Tracey is beside me, looking at me questioningly.

'Oh, no, I was just – thinking.'

'Well, you're staring into space. Are you crossing the road, or what?'

We both take a big leap at the same time and jump the pile of slush. Laughing, we cross the street together.

'It's turning to rain.' She shudders. 'Meant to get warmer.' A slight frown creases her brow. 'You look slightly out of it, if you don't mind me saying so.'

'Oh, it's the season,' I say, flippantly. 'Busiest time of the year in my line of work.'

'Oh, right.'

'You should come to a service,' I tell her.

'You should come horse riding,' she responds, smartly.

I'm taken aback. 'Why?'

'Looks to me like you need a stress-buster.' She raises her perfectly plucked eyebrows. 'Best thing for anyone who wants to let go and leave it all behind. Take a horse out.'

'Do I look *that* stressed?'

'Honestly? You always look a bit anxious. But today – yes.'

I feel as if someone's punched me in the stomach. *I always look a bit anxious? Do I?*

'I've been ill,' I say, and it seems a lame excuse.

She ignores it, anyway. 'If you want a bit of stress relief, come riding. I won't even charge you. I'm free tomorrow lunchtime. What do you say?'

'Oh, I don't think . . .'

'I'm not asking you out!' she says, brusquely.

'No, I know—'

'Do you always run away from challenges?'

She's very persistent. I stare at her, perplexed. *Barny runs away. I don't run away.* My stomach turns over. *Do I?*

'Alright,' I say. 'Challenge accepted. But I warn you, I'm not a great rider. Done it a few times, but to be honest, I'm better on bikes. They've got brakes.'

'If the weather's OK, come down to the stables at twelve. I've got a nice, slow old horse for you.' She smirks a bit. 'It'll be fun!'

Fun? Well, maybe I could do with some of that. Forgiveness, running away, doubt. I've dealt with it all. And yes . . . I've lived it all.

I'm eating toast with too much butter on it, and reading my emails. The one from Meg is heavily detailed. She's spoken to Micky on the phone, told her how sorry she is, arranged a time to meet. *Do you have to see her? Can't you just . . .* I stop myself from following that train of thought. *Jason! Get a grip.*

Micky is five months' pregnant, and she and her husband have split up. No hope of reconciliation. She seems more concerned with her life now than she ever is about the past. Meg has lived this for two years or more, but Micky hasn't. Meg finds it hard to get her head around the fact that it appears the betrayal – Meg's affair with Micky's fiancé – has been so much more important to her than it has been for her friend. She wants to talk about the past, but Micky seems reluctant. Meg's going to see her tomorrow, meet her face to face. Not a word about Nun's Drift. She talks about helping to pick up the pieces; she cares about Micky's wellbeing; she may need to 'be there' . . .

Meg! I take a moment to breathe. Then I type a short answer that I hope sounds objective: *Pray about it. Remember God speaks in the silence.*

I should take my own advice. I rarely sit in the quiet, and yet I know silence restores and refreshes me. I really am such a hypocrite.

She signs off with a personal touch: *You're such a good friend, Jason.*

Good friend?

My finger is poised over the keyboard. *When are you coming back?* I delete that sentence. Time to get ready for a challenge.

I'm riding a skewbald mare that Ally calls 'the armchair' because, apparently, it's so comfortable – although I know I'm going to be sore tomorrow. Still, it's been worth coming out. Ally points towards distant woods, saying there was an old house, long since demolished, and a remaining bridge where the river widens, which originally led to the fine mansion. She says the bridge now seems to lead to nowhere. *Hmm.*

We're on a little hill just outside of Nun's Drift. There's been a thaw, and a watery winter sun illuminates the view. The remnant of snow is lying deep in ditches, and in the colder places which don't receive the warmth of sunlight. I'm amazed how quickly a rise in temperature has cleared most of it away.

The village looks beautiful from this vantage point. There's a footpath over the hill leading down into the meadows below, and I determine to walk it soon. Nun's Drift would look lovely from here in the first flush of spring, quiet and content in the middle of greening fields and the first bright leaves. For some reason, I wouldn't expect Ally to be so poetic but she's describing buttercups that smother the hill in late April, and the abundance of wild white violets, and where they can be found. She tells me that the name of this place is 'Chosen Hill'.

Chosen.

I don't want to move on, and Ally must realise that because she doesn't move either.

'It's perfect,' I say at last. 'Like a picture.'

'Yes. The village looks different further away.' Then she observes, 'Sometimes people are better from a distance. Don't you think so?'

'Well . . . they get messier close up.'

Silence descends and it suddenly feels sacred. From here, St Saviour's, on the opposite hill, looks so far away, but it isn't really. It's just some fields and a couple of streets off. *God's not as far away as we think.*

I feel him speak in the quiet. *Sometimes it's about getting a fresh perspective. Just looking at things from a different point of view.* My horse shifts, and I feel something in myself shift too. *Our view can be skewed. God sees things as they really are.*

Ally points, suddenly, and I watch a heron rise from the shining stream below. It's a huge bird, flapping its great wings in no hurry. I feel my own agenda flapping away with the bird. Time to release everything to God, and let him write the next chapter.

'Glad you came?' asks Ally.

'Gladder than you know.' I turn in my saddle. 'Do you really think people are better from a distance?'

'Yes, mostly.' She shrugs in a nonchalant way. 'But some are alright up close . . . I suppose.' She glances at me briefly, but doesn't keep eye contact. 'I might come to church at Christmas,' she says, coolly, patting her horse's dappled neck.

'Good to see you're up for a challenge.'

She looks at me, ironically.

We turn the horses to go back to the yard. Suddenly, I know that my life really is useful, right here, right now.

There's a point to it all. A bigger story. And you're part of it, Jason. My heart lifts.

The Sunday before Christmas I'm speaking on 'joy'. I smile. That's a sermon I could preach today.

An Ending
Meg

I can't stay with Micky – laying down my life in some sort of penance, helping, being there for her . . . The thought had crossed my mind, but now, as the last wisps of the smokescreen clears, I finally see things as they really are. She doesn't need me. No bitterness, no recrimination, but not a lot of warmth either.

Initially, I feared her parents' reaction, but their eyes – once so kind and loving, then accusing and angry – are vacant as soon as they see me. I'm an inconvenience, not part of it; they have a grandchild coming, and a much-loved lost sheep has returned to the fold. They're throwing a party in their hearts. I'm not invited.

I don't really figure in Micky's life. Frustratingly, she put off our meeting several times, with various excuses. Now that I'm actually here, I apologise again, but she blithely remarks that 'it was all so long ago'. Anyway, that guy – does she actually struggle to remember his name, or is she pretending? – she hadn't really *loved* him. Did I ever think she did? Her voice is flippant.

She's had another life these past two and a half years. They'd met and married within six weeks; he'd proposed – 'with a gorgeous ring' – after only five days ... in Italy, so exciting. *Well, Micky. You always did want to get married.* It was amazing at the start, but it's all gone wrong; he's decided that he's 'not ready for a baby', and she's realised he isn't the right man after all.

I find it hard to speak. 'It was awful,' I say at last, 'when you disappeared. You came off your socials ... I didn't know if ... well, no one could find you.'

'I didn't *want* to be found,' she says, shortly. Now, pregnant and alone, she does.

I feel a sudden wave of anger. 'I thought you were dead.'

She actually laughs. 'Well, I'm not. As you can see.'

Micky, how could you be so selfish? Do you know what I went through? What your parents have suffered? Don't I matter? Doesn't anyone, apart from you? I don't say anything, though; because I see it. Charming, captivating – damaged. Micky's like the rest of us. Messed up.

I speak to her about God, about faith. She mentions she's into crystals, and shows me some.

'I prayed for you,' I tell her.

She stares at me blankly. 'Why?'

There's no connection; I feel as if I don't know her anymore. I force the idea of 'rebound' into the back of my mind. I got it wrong, selfishly wrong, but I'm not responsible for further choices. We all get to choose how we react to wrongs, don't we?

She talks about her husband, tells me his faults; a studied, careless coldness masks deep disappointment. Then she says she's tired, and 'let's keep in touch', but when I turn at the garden gate, the door is already shut.

I'm sorry, Micky.

And I forgive you, too.

I go back to Dad's. Wandering up the path to the familiar block of flats, I glance up at the window and see him waiting.

I take the stairs. The door to number 15 is already cracked open. I remove my shoes and pad into the living room. Dad's there, his face full of concern. I hug him tightly.

'I'm going home. To Nun's Drift.' I sink into the big red velour sofa. Dad's face breaks into a knowing smile as he hands me a big mug of tea.

I'll pack my stuff later. My bag will be heavy. But I won't be carrying any extra luggage.

It's nearly Christmas, and I come away from Dad's feeling lighter with each passing mile. As the train rocks towards Nun's Drift, I see tracks separating, and the distance growing between me and the past.

Now, as I arrive at the station at Howfield Cross, I feel as if I'm stepping into a new phase of my life, just as I step onto the platform.

I take a deep breath. *You know, I've even missed those bells . . .*

I expect to see my aunt's old Land Rover waiting for me, so I'm surprised to see a van instead, and a familiar figure leaning against it.

'What are you doing here?' I ask.

'Complaining already?'

'Amazed you're still around.'

'Are you?' He waves his cigarette in the air. 'Haven't given it up.'

'Some things never change.'

He stubs the cigarette out, glancing at me sideways as he opens the driver's door. 'You never know. I might surprise you yet.'

You think? Ha! I'm one step ahead of you, Barny Baines!

Barny

I'm late. I'm looking for my phone. I put it down in here somewhere. Where? And why I am so worked up? It's not a date. We're just going to church. *Church!*

I move the bag off the battered old chair by the wardrobe. There's the phone, slipped down the side . . .

I look at the bag. Packed and ready to leave. I'm always doing it; I pack it. I unpack it. I pack it again. I run my hand through my hair. *Just unpack it, Barny, put the stuff away. You know you're staying for a while.* I'll sort it tomorrow.

Tomorrow . . . Christmas Day! A meal with Jason and a few of the lads who are on their own. Meg asked me to have dinner with her and the family, but it doesn't seem right. Not this year, anyway. I sit down abruptly on the bed. *Am I really thinking I'll be here next Christmas?* Well, who knows. I blame Jason. Old Dazzles. He's got a way with words. I blame Meg too. Meg . . . And that twinkle.

I think back to earlier this week. I was doing a job at Tony's – yes, he employs me now, just a few jobs here and there that he's too busy or too cranky to do himself. Or maybe he considers me a sort of new friend; bizarre. I feel as if I'm right back in that huge old kitchen with the bad condensation dripping down the windows. I see myself wiping my hands on a rag when Cornelia walked in. I hadn't seen her for ages. I did a double take. Something was different. She'd seemed older, somehow. *She's cut her hair, that's it.* Yes, but more than that—

'Hey,' I'd said, at last. 'How're you doing?'

'Great.' She'd opened the fridge, reached for some juice.

'I hear you're at college now.'

'Yep.' She'd poured some juice into a glass. I'd noticed she didn't offer me any.

I'd cleared my throat. Something had been on my mind for a while. 'You know,' I'd said, lightly, 'I never did have a *thing* with Ally.'

'What?' She'd stared at me, then, as if she didn't understand what I was talking about.

'Well, you know . . .' My voice had dwindled into silence.

'You take care of yourself, Barny, alright?' With those words, coolly chucked in my direction, she'd left the kitchen.

I'd watched her leave and felt sudden regret, which surprised me. Then I'd frowned. I'd had a feeling she hadn't known I was there before she came in. Or maybe she did? It seemed as if she didn't know what I meant about Ally. But surely . . .

I'd realised then that I was still wiping my hands. I'd thrown the rag down.

Ah well.

Now, here in this bedroom, I get up and stretch. Phone, keys, cigarettes. Time to go.

Rosemary

'That young vicar's not so bad, you know,' says Arthur.

'Yes, I do know that!' I wrap my new fawn cashmere scarf round my neck. *Daisy Parker's clothes are pricey, but my word, they're lovely.*

'He's pretty good with a spade. You should have seen him shovelling snow for old Alec. I appreciated that.'

Old Alec! He's not a lot older than you, Arthur!

'Rosey! Doorbell. Your lift's here.'

I want to ask if he's coming with me, but I don't. *Maybe one day. Who knows.*

I smile to myself. I'm off to Midnight Mass. What would Anne and Gordon say? Actually, they've gone. Mrs Fordham phoned me to say a removal van had been seen outside their house. 'Off to the next upgrade, I suppose,' she'd said, but her tone was very dry.

I know it's not very godly, but I'd felt like waving flags when they left the village. Still, I'd been generous, and given them the flags when they'd asked for them. In fact, I'd marched round there in the dead of night and left them, like a couple of sentries, either side of the front door. I'd found that quite amusing. Even going out in the dark as if I was on a secret mission was rather exciting. In fact, I'm finding life in general a lot more fun than I used to.

Meg's back. I'm pleased about that. I've missed her. She came home yesterday, and even popped in for a cup of tea. She brought me a box of chocolates. I shouldn't have eaten any, but I've nearly polished off the whole lot. I really do need to go on a diet in the new year.

She told me a few snippets of Micky's new life. Meg doesn't show her feelings easily, but I can see she's hurt; she's trying to hide it. I'd had less than positive thoughts about Micky, but I did feel a bit vindicated that I hadn't got it wholly wrong. *I really didn't like that girl.* I sigh. I'm so not perfect; I've got a long way to go.

I wonder if Jason would like me to make some flags? So useful in worship. And I wonder what he'd think if I asked if we could start a little home group, with me, and Flora, and Daisy? I've been spending time with Daisy since she's been poorly, and I believe she'd quite like to know a bit more about the Good Shepherd.

'Rosey! Your lift's waiting.'

'Oh, yes – I was just thinking.'

Arthur squeezes my hand and gives me a peck on the cheek.

'Don't drink too much mulled wine.'

I throw my arms around his neck and give him a proper kiss.

'I love you,' I say.

'I love you too, Rosey. I'll wait up for you. Alright?'

Jason

Midnight Mass! The church is heaving. The candles are lit and the whole place is filled with a soft light. I glance up at the lofty wooden ceiling, and wonder if there are angels hovering, waiting for the service to begin. *Well, there are certainly bats.* I smile, and look around at the people in the pews.

Old Alec is there. He's chatting to Flora. He looks quite animated. Do I detect some flirting? Flora's face is flushed, like a young girl's. I spot Ian from the Thompson-Traceys', sitting with his fiancée; I wonder if he'll ever stop holding her hand. Maybe he's afraid she'll fly away if he lets go.

Tony's here, looking uncomfortable in a smart jacket and tie, sitting beside Louisa; she seems very at ease, talking with Mrs Fordham. I give him a wink, and he manages an embarrassed grin. Signing up for the pre-marriage counselling course was a big step for him, and he's agreed to attend meetings around his addiction. I hope it's the beginning of some sort of breakthrough in his life. It'll be interesting to see what happens next. Then I think about Cornelia; she never comes to church. I need to seriously pray for her.

All of a sudden, I hear Tony's voice in my mind: 'Everyone wants a family, don't they? Somewhere they belong?'

Yes. *And this is my family. I belong.*

Meg walks in, and my heart almost stops. Barny is right behind her. They sit together. I take a deep breath, and then wander over to them.

'Well, I made it,' he says. 'At last.'

'About time.' I shake his hand warmly.

He squirms on the pew. 'Seats are a bit hard.'

So were you. But I think there's a bit of a softening these days.

Meg looks at me, and I look at her.

I've missed you, Meg. Really missed you . . .

Smiling, I nod to her – and turn away.

Rosemary bustles in, pointing out the Good Shepherd window to the dark-haired girl beside her. Ally's staring up, curiosity evident on her face.

'So, you took the challenge?' I say.

'Well, *you* did,' she replies, wrinkling her nose a little. 'So why not?'

I laugh. 'Yes, why not!'

As I go to the front, I remember what I told Meg when I first met her: Nun's Drift . . . *Something healing in the fabric of this place.* I'm not sure if that was 'just words' back then, intuition, or the romance of this beautiful village; but now my heart soars as I realise it's true. We're a community, living one day at a time, focusing on the Good Shepherd. Like liquorice allsorts, we're all different, but all in the bag together; each with our own sorrows and joys, our true hearts known only to God.

'Welcome!' I smile at the expectant faces. 'Welcome to you all!'

About the Author

Sheila Jacobs is a writer, editor and award-winning author of twenty titles (to date). She writes fiction and non-fiction. She has been involved in the Christian publishing industry for more than twenty years as a freelance editor. She enjoys working with new and experienced authors, encouraging them in their writing journey through developmental editing, tips, advice and author mentoring. She is also a speaker, and a workshop and retreat leader (writing and inspirational).

Find out more about Sheila and her work by visiting her website at www.sheila-jacobs.co.uk

Also by Sheila Jacobs

Watchers

ISBN: 978-1-912863-67-9

A Little Book of Rest

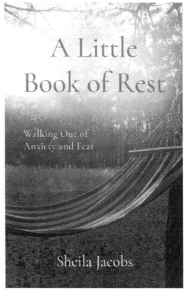

ISBN: 978-1-915046-03-1

For more information scan the code below